HAMMURABI

ROAD

A Tale of Northern Ontario

Railroad Vengeance

By

Steve Vernon

Stark Raven Press

What readers say about STEVE VERNON

"Vernon manages to wrap up about six varieties of weird in the pages of HAMMURABI ROAD." – Gef Fox, WAG THE FOX BLOG

"Steve Vernon is a hard writer to pin down. And that's a good thing." – Blu Gilliand, DARK SCRIBE MAGAZINE

"Armed with a bizarre sense of humor, a huge amount of originality, a flair for taking risks and a strong grasp of characterization – Steve Vernon's got the chops for sure!" – James Beach, DARK DISCOVERIES MAGAZINE

"If Harlan Ellison, Richard Matheson and Robert Bloch had a three-way sex romp in a hot tub, and then a team of scientists came in and filtered out the water and mixed the leftover DNA into a test tube, the resulting genetic experiment would most likely grow up into Steve Vernon." – Slade Grayson BOOKGASM

"Only a handful of horror authors can make me wring my hands in anticipation of their newest release. Steve Vernon is at the top of the list." – T.T. Zuma, HORROR WORLD

"Steve Vernon was born to write. He's the real deal and we're lucky to have him." - Richard Chizmar, editor/publisher/boss of CEMETERY DANCE MAGAZINE

Hammurabi Road
Author: Steve Vernon

ISBN-13: 978-1-927765-10-4

First Printing – August 30, 2013

If you can read this novella without cracking a grin you ought to run and see a dentist – because your mouth must be seriously broken.

Dedication

To my brother Dan

Who told me about railroading

from the inside out.

"You never let me down."

HAMMURABI ROAD

THE MOON WAS A STONE'S THROW away from the Jack Pine Stretch and the lights of the town were nothing but a distant memory and the three of us were bunched together in the front seat of the pickup on account of the back seat being crammed full of Tyree. He was kicking up some, trying to shuck himself out of the duct tape, snare wire and rope we'd tangled him up in, but other than that he wasn't making much of a sound. The gag helped some and the fear of possible retribution did the rest.

"Moose are the worst," I said.

"Worse than cows?" Donny asked.

The thing about Donny was he didn't always care about hearing the answer. To him talking was a little like table tennis. The object of the game was to snap that ball right back at the other guy just as fast and as hard as you can. Donny had an incurable habit of asking questions because it pretty well guaranteed an answer. Words just felt good coming out of his mouth, I guess. I didn't mind. Donny looked up to me and made no secret about it. I did my best to live up to his respect. Bert and Ernie couldn't have done it any better.

"Worse than bears," I said. "Usually a moose will just bounce, but man alive when they get their hooves tangled up in the tracks the engine will drag them a mile before letting go. You've got to hose their carcasses out of the locomotive's wheel trucks. I'm telling you that nothing stinks like dead moose. Not even Irvin."

Donny liked that. He grinned me that Donny smile of his, half-cocked to one side, all bright and innocent. Looking at that Donny smile I knew that nothing could ever change between us. Donny and I were arguing about what kind of track-kill stank the worst after it had been pile-driver-pureed by a half a mile of freight train. It happened more often than you might think.

"You're sure about that, are you?" Donny asked.

"Sure as shooting," I replied.

"Shooting isn't sure," Donny pointed out. "Sometimes people miss."

Donny had a point in his own weird kind of way. That was Donny's magic. He wasn't slow or retarded or whatever you want to call it. He just had a different way of looking at things, was all.

"You know what I mean Donny."

"I know what you figure you mean, but you're only guessing. There are three sides to every story," Donny said. "Yours, mine and the truth."

I smiled and nodded, preferring not to argue, but I did know what I was talking about. In my twenty years of railroading I had shoveled and swept and hosed more track-kill from off of the CNR rails than the rest of this pickup truck combined, including Tyree. There was something magnetic in those rails that called for the kill more surely than the north wind calls the wandering wild goose home.

"Do you think there are any bears out here?" Donny asked nervously.

Donny gets antsy when you mention bears, even the Winnie the Pooh stuffed kind. He's got what you might call a history with bears.

"All of the bears will be down to the town dump by now, feeding off of the weekend leavings," I said. "And here we are out here, missing the show."

It was as true as train tracks.

The bears hang around down at the old town dump and waited all week for the garbage trucks to roll in with something good to eat. It was easy pickings, sure, but I think it was also just something for them to do. Just the same way we'd go up there to the dump on the weekends and watch the bears picking through the garbage. Sometimes life was just a way of making the time go past.

Donny had his own way of passing the time. He used to go down to the dump with a pellet rifle when he was a kid and even older, taking pot-shots at the bears. He liked to plink those bears with his bee-bee's, figuring they were so damn big they couldn't even feel it. Except one day one of them bears took it into its shaggy mind to prove Donny wrong. I never saw a grown man climb a tree so fast. Too bad the bear could climb too. If I hadn't pulled the pickup truck under the tree while Donny jumped for it the story might have ended up with what was left of Donny coming out of the bear's asshole in slow dark chunks. Ever since then Donny just didn't care much for bears.

I guess I could understand that, just fine.

"Dead skunk smells worse than bear," Donny looked nervously out the window, as if he expected Smokey the Bear to come running up from out of the darkness to break the window glass with a well-swung shovel. "Way worse. Don't you think so, Irvin?"

"Shut up and let me drive," Irvin said, speed-jittering his Players filterless from one corner of his mouth to the other and back in an irritating kind of fuck-you-and-the-caboose-you-rode-in-on way. Irvin was like that. Dead focused on the task at hand. He didn't care for distractions of any sort, which was understandable given that we were driving down a dirt trail in the dark of a moonless night with our headlights turned off. That Irvin had good eyes, I guess. He leaned right over the steering wheel, his face practically jammed up against the windshield glass, just staring into the darkness and driving at it straight on.

"What the hell are you steering by?" I asked. "You sure as shit can't see a thing."

"I can see the starlight glinting off of the rail tracks," Irvin said. "That's all of the compass that I'll ever need."

I looked hard. It was true. You could see the rails glinting in the darkness. I guess the trail was always there if you looked hard enough for something to follow. Maybe that's what the railroad tracks were for. To let us know where we were going and where we had been.

"I still think a cow is worse," Donny said. "When their guts blow up and all of that fart gas honks out. I seen two cows get it once, up around west of Wawa. They were humping on the track and I guess they didn't hear the train coming. They got creamed while they were creaming. Pretty damn funny, I think."

"Wouldn't that have been a bull and a cow?" I asked. "If they were doing what I think they were doing?"

"I don't know," Donny said with a shrug. "Maybe they were lesbian cows."

I nodded. It almost made sense if you didn't stop too long to think about it. Most things did.

"Scratch a cow, find a lesbian," Irvin observed. "Pretty girls put it out the best."

Irvin was always the deep thinker of our bunch. We weren't always sure what he was talking about most of the time – but you could bet that it was DEEP!

The three of us had been together since we were kids. Irvin had six years on us, but he'd flunked grade twelve twice before his old man got him hooked up on the section gang. Irvin learned a whole lot more from diesel and steel than he ever learned in school. He followed the rails and he never looked back.

"Man, there's nothing worse than cow farts," Donny said. "They stink like rotten grass gas."

"Rotten ass grass gas," I suggested, stringing one more box car onto his line.

"Rotten ass grass gas, passing fast," Donny elaborated, with a silly little giggle. Then we both started to laugh. It wasn't that funny, but the giggling and the gag-cracking helped keep our minds off of what we were getting set to do.

"I'm trying to drive here," Irvin announced, in a louder than usual voice. "Do you fellows mind holding it down, or am I going to have duct tape the two of you shut up as well?"

We both shut up. Not that we usually listened all that hard to what Irvin had to say, but we both knew what he was thinking about. It had been our buddies, who had died in that Hammer Abbey Hotel fire, and we had plenty to beef about with Tyree for setting the blaze, but it had been Irvin's big brother Gilbert who died there as well. Blood counted more than anybody's buddy in any book you cared to name, and some that had no name at all.

There wasn't proof that Tyree did it, but the whole town knew it as a fact. Tyree had been royally pissed at the hotel ever since they threw him out for scratching up the snooker table the time he used a leaf rake for a pool cue. So I guess everybody just plain figured that

Tyree had set the fire, and that was all the judge and jury we needed in these here parts.

The real truth was that most folks just didn't care for Tyree's family. You see, Tyree came from Norman Township, where the roads were all dirt and you got your water from an iron pump. That wasn't all that bad in itself. In fact the fact was nearly half of the local crew came from Norman township, but Tyree's family came from the side of Norman that folks on the other side of Norman loved to talk about the most, the wrong side of the wrong side of the tracks, so when somebody dumped a couple of quarts of gasoline in the backroom of the Hammer Abbey Railroad Hotel and threw in a lit book of matches after it, Tyree was the first usual suspect to be considered.

Now the Hammer Abbey wasn't that much as hotels went. The rooms were small and you could smell what your neighbour ate for his supper at 3am in the morning when the night farts kicked in, but it was where the traveling men would hang their hats. The rooms were cheap and fairly clean and it was ice cube handy to the bootlegger's shack. So when it went up in blazes folks around here decided that they'd miss it.

Still, there wasn't all that much in the way of material evidence so the courts and the cops didn't do much about it. The police just shrugged and Pontius Pilated their donut-stained hands into the air. Life moved on and the sun kept going up and down and the trains kept rolling.

So it was up to us.

We drove on in silence for a minute or two. That was about as long of a silence as Donny could hold on to.

"Cow farts are bad," Donny allowed. "A piggery smells worse, though. You ever drive past one?"

"There's a pig farm out by Coniston," I said. "You can smell the damn thing for miles."

"Ain't that funny?" Donny said. "Pig shit smells so bad but bacon smells so good. How's that work, you figure?"

"It's the smoke that does it," I allowed. "They smoke and salt the pork. That smoke drives all of the pig shit out of meat, I reckon."

"I wish to hell somebody would smoke and salt you, Hanny," Irvin growled. "Maybe that'd do something about all of the shit you're so full of."

That was my name, Hanny. It was short for Hanlan, my grandpa's name. My folks gave the name to me back when I was born and unable to protect myself from such abuses, figuring I could hold onto it after grandpa finally died. That's how it worked in our family. Names were handed down like old clothes in a kind of living memorial. Just as soon as somebody grew out of one name somebody else got to wear it.

I figured on saving my money and buying myself a brand new name someday. I had in mind something snazzy, like Trick Magnet H. Flash, but first I figured I'd better learn how to rap. I figured that if I could just change my name it might just change my entire life outlook. I might grow a longer dick, and go up a whole tax bracket, and maybe even bag me a cheerleader or two.

"I smoked Labrador tea once," Donny said. "It didn't do a thing for me. I never tried smoking bacon before."

"You're not supposed to smoke Labrador tea," I said. "You drink it. It's good for farts, not that you need any help in that department. Your back door works just fine and dandy."

It was true. Given enough hard boiled eggs and home brewed beer Donny could single-handedly lay down a counter-barrage on any Saturday bean supper you cared to name. It was kind of his calling in life. The man was made of methane and had a low and sonorous fart tone that always reminded me of a foghorn sounding out, somewhere far out to sea. The sound of his flatulence gave him a kind of a mysterious appeal that was strangely lost on most of the women we tried to hang around.

"Well I smoked that Labrador Tea just the same," Donny said. "On account of Billy Three-Legs Tootoosis told me I could. I smoked it and then I said I was sorry, because Billy Three-Legs Tootoosis said that you had to apologize to anything that you killed in this life, even if it was only a tea bush."

"Ha," I laughed. "If Billy Three-Legs Tootoosis tells you that shit is ham, are you going to fry yourself up a turd and slide it on in between two slices of fresh buttered bread?"

Billy Three-Legs Tootoosis was our town's resident Indian. It was an honorary position and Billy took it as seriously as if it were something big like the Nobel Peace Prize or the Stanley Cup. People would point at him and make jokes about him. He was kind of upholding a tradition representing the kind of backwoods stereotype that let folks imagine that things didn't really ever need to change.

"Who else would they tell their racist jokes about?" Billy Three-Legs Tootoosis had asked me once after I'd asked him if being the town Indian bothered him any. "I figure I'm taking one for the tribes. So long as I keep grinning and taking it nobody else gets that racist Indian crap dumped on them."

The truth was, most of the real Indians around here preferred to stay on the reservations. They just didn't want to live anywhere close to town on account of the kind of people who lived in towns. Speaking as somebody who lived in town, I figured there was no accounting for taste, I guess.

"Billy Three-Legs Tootoosis is part-Cree," Donny said. "He told me so. He knows a lot about the wilderness and things."

"Billy Three-Legs Tootoosis knows shit," I said. "The closest he ever got to the reservation was all those lonely Saturday nights he spent playing tepee with his wickiup in the back seat of his grandma's Ford pick-up truck."

"Do you girls mind shutting up?" Irvin was plainly pissed. "I got something more important on my mind than the fiddling proclivities of Billy Three-Legged's never-to-be-trusted right hand."

Irvin didn't take his eyes off of the trail ahead, he just laid a track out for us to follow; a trail as cold and hard as frozen turds.

"I can still smell that goddamn Hammer Abbey hotel smoke," he said, and we all knew what he was talking about. "And it isn't from any goddamn Labrador tea. I smelled it three goddamn weeks ago and so did you two, if I recollect correctly. And I can still smell it reeking off of that goddamned sad bastard stretched out in our backseat."

"Goddamn, Irvin," I said, trying to lighten the mood. "That's four goddamns in as many sentences. That's got to be some kind of goddamn record. Are you fixing on starting up your own goddamn religion?"

"Why the goddamn hell not?" Irvin asked. "Maybe I will. Call it the High Holy Tracklayers Bullshit-Flinging Church of the One-Eyed Pig-Fuckers complete with clog dancing and free liquor every Saturday night. I reckon it'd beat the hell out of what that old boy upstairs has been dishing out."

It was well said, but I couldn't believe any of what I was hearing. Firstly, I was amazed that Irvin had thought of a name that out-did Trick Magnet H. Flash, but secondly I couldn't believe that somebody could speak so sacrilegiously in the middle of what we were up to.

"Don't tell me you've got a grudge against God?" I said. "Irvin, I know you can get pissy, but how in the hell can you get worked up about somebody we only talk about once a week, excepting hockey season?"

"Just because we don't talk about him, doesn't mean he isn't still hanging over our heads, nosing into our business and butt-fucking our destinies."

"Damn it Irvin," I said. "You could say that about the Prime Minister or the President and you'd be just as right. Why pick on God? He's a good old boy, hung his son on a cross and all that happy puck-shit."

"Do you think so?" Irvin asked. "I've been hearing about how good and kind and merciful that old boy is upstairs, but I've read the Old Testament. You just take a look at all the folks that Jehovah decreed needed to be burned and sacked and smited out of their homes. That old fellow is a psychopathic serial killer, you just check the facts."

"I like cereal ever since I was a kid," Donny said. "Especially the sugary kind, but not Captain Crunch. I like my cereal soggy."

Irvin and I both ignored Donny. Sometimes that boy just insisted on driving in the wrong direction on the wrong side of the road using the Saturday funny pages for a road map.

"Irvin, those are just bible stories," I said. "They don't mean anything."

"They're parables is what they are," Irvin said. "The preacher will read them to you once a week at Sunday school, trying to indoctrinate you into their way of thinking. It's like brainwashing, only dirtier. You got to face up to the facts, Hanny. What happened in the before colors the here and now like permanent oil paint."

"Indoctrinate," I said, going for a grin. "That's a real good word, Irvin. You look that up in your Reader's Digest?"

But Irvin wasn't in a grinning mood.

"That's the trouble with you, Hanny. You look at me and all you can see is dumb old Irvin, but I'm a whole lot smarter than you'd think. You can't go on just an appearance. House paint and home improvements don't mean shit."

Here it comes, I thought. Irvin hardly ever said anything, except when he wanted to say a whole lot.

He kept on talking. I figured he'd run out of steam soon enough, but you never could tell with Irvin. Usually he said so very little, that when he started it was kind of like he had to empty out what ever crap he'd been holding back.

"That's the whole problem. Folks are just relying on what they hear about this old fellow God. They look at the pictures and they see this big old Santa Claus-like looking fellow leaning down out of a cloud and cum-showering us with milk and honey and manna-o-manna and they figure he's no worse than Grandpa Walton."

Oh shit. Irvin was getting set to filibuster.

"Well what's so bad about God?" I asked. I knew I was opening a door to a diatribe, but if I didn't open that door he was just going to kick it down all the same and talk all the more. I was his friend. It was part of my job to hear out all of his bullshit, no matter how irritating it got to be. So I let him let it fly, figuring maybe he had a point. Besides, I never did truly trust Will Geer.

Irvin pointed his favorite rude finger straight up at the truck cab's roof.

"I'll tell you what's wrong. Where was that old bastard when this peanut-fart dumped gasoline all over the back room of the Hammer Abbey Railroad Hotel? Where was he when Gil was sucking smoke and chewing on hot cinders? Where was he when the bolts gave way on that rusty old fire escape that should have been replaced back when Christ wore short pants. Where was we when they were hanging out of the windows like fucking Christmas decorations? Where was he and what the fuck was he thinking?"

"Are you done?" I asked.

"Just about," He answered.

With that Irvin bounced the pick-up over a rut that I swore he drove straight through on purpose. I left a Hanny-sized dent in the top of the pick-up can and Tyree bounced hard off of the back seat and wedged down onto the floorboards of the truck. Next thing you know he was jammed down hard and he was making strangled scared noises like he was trying breath through the mud-stained upholstery, which I guess he was.

"Fish him up out of there before he chokes to death," Irvin ordered. "Smothering is just too damned easy for this bastard. I want him to pay for what he done, old school Hammurabi-style. An eye for an asshole, fucker. God has spoken."

Donny and I turned around and reached over the ridge of the seat backs to try and haul Tyree up. It was an awkward enough stunt, bellying over the seat backs and reaching down to pick up somebody who didn't want to be picked up. What made it harder was Irvin didn't even bother slowing the truck down.

Tyree didn't help matters any once he started kicking and bucking like a freshly landed muskellunge.

"Stop that bastard's kicking before he dents up the track cab," Irvin commanded. "I've got one dry nerve left and that rotten eyed prick with ears is pissing all over it."

Right about then a part of me wanted to ask Irvin just when the hell he was going to stop giving us orders and start giving us a hand, but the part of me that stays away from meat run green and dating close cousins decided to shut up for a while and just say nothing. Irvin was a bad man on a good day and tonight was no time to be fucking around.

I reached down for Tyree but in the dark I was grabbing at the wrong end. He jammed his boots up against my hand, catching all four of my fingers against the side of the truck. I invented a few creative new names for Jesus and all of his saints and a couple of trailer park angels, all the while trying to rise philosophically above the pain.

Which was right about the time that Tyree chewed his mouth clear of the duct tape gag we had wrapped across his lips and sank his dirty uncolgated yellow teeth into the knuckle-hinges of Donny's left hand.

Donny let out a noise that sounded a little like Whitney Houston stump-fucking a three year old beagle hound. While Donny was working on the high notes Tyree stomped at my other hand and I sang out in harmony. The Vienna Philharmonic Boys Neutron Choir didn't have a good goddamn thing on us, for sure.

Which was right about the time that we hit the bear.

* 2 *

NOW THE BEARS AROUND THESE HERE PARTS just aren't that much to speak of. I mean, we're not talking Jeremiah Johnson "can-you-skin-griz?" kind of grizzly bears here. We're just looking at a bunch of fat old flea-bitten black bears, the welfare bums of the ursine kingdom. You see your average black bear is a whole lot more scared of us humans than we might be scared of them.

Usually.

Part of it comes down to size. If you're looking at a grizzly you're talking about something that can weigh in at over a thousand pounds and stands about ten feet tall, just built for looming and tearing apart whoever happens to be standing before them. Your usual Northern Ontario black bear isn't much bigger than your average St. Bernard. He's built more for rooting around old dead crap, hunting up grubs and garbage and anthills and road kill. They only stand at about four feet tall hunkered down, which is the posture you usually see them in. The black bear's haunches don't allow them much in the way of standing up straight, unless they're pulling themselves up on a tree or a rock or a pick-up truck like ours.

That old bear come up over that truck like he was meaning to, hitting face first against the windshield and spraying the glass with a big frothy gust of bear spit and fresh blood. We must have hit the bastard head on. It looked like he'd been running at us, like he figured he could take us down.

Maybe he could.

Irvin stomped on the brakes while his own face was smashing itself up against the windshield glass. For a moment it looked like the two of them, bear and man, were trying to rub themselves cheek to cheek against the hardened glass in a weird kind of Yogi-Bear-Brokeback moment.

I had a pretty good eyeball of the whole sordid proceedings, being flung forward like I was from leaning over the seat back trying to catch hold of Tyree, and then being pitched backwards and lambasting the rear curve of my skull against the dashboard. I remember seeing a cigarette burn mark right beside my right cheekbone, charred into the vinyl of the dash where somebody had crushed out a cigarette. The burn mark looked a little like the shape of Italy, like a boot, you know? At that moment in time it seemed like the most important thing in the world was for me to remember just what sort of shape that cigarette burn looked like.

Donny was lying flat on top of my back, and he was still hanging on to Tyree. Or rather, Tyree was hanging onto Donny's hand with his teeth. The momentum of the collision had hauled Tyree up from under the seat. He wiggled himself up over the seat backs, moving pretty spry for a fellow bound with rope and wire and duct tape. Then he caterpillar-humped his way up over Donny and me, planted his boots against the angle of the front seat and sprung-kicked himself straight out through the already bear-broken windshield.

I don't quite know where he figured he was going to get to, launching himself that way, but it was a pretty goddamned impressive sight I've got to tell you. We're talking scud missiles and catapulting burning bushes. He went up through that windshield glass like he was part Evel Knievel and part John Shaft. Mind you, the bear had weakened the window considerably.

"Get hold of that hot fingered, light footed asshole," Irvin shouted, trying to haul himself free from his seat belt. By now Irvin's face was war-painted with his own blood and at that particular moment he looked a whole lot more native than Billy Three-Legs Tootoosis could have hoped to look like following a month of Indian sunburns and Tonto freestyle rap lessons.

I reached out my arm like a JC Pentecostal on the cross, and wrapped my stoved-up fingers around the door handle. Then I jacked the handle up and felt the mechanism unlatch, but with Donny still spread-eagled across my backbone, I couldn't do much more than hold the door open just wide enough to let a few more bloodthirsty Northern Ontario mosquitoes into the truck cab to feed upon our freshly spilled vitality.

Next thing I knew I felt Donny's boots going up and over my backbone like it was a stepladder, and he's going right up over the bear's head, trying to catch hold of our runaway arsonist.

I had to give the boy credit. He might have been a few beers short of a six-pack, but he was never much backward when it comes to going straight forward. If something needed doing, Donny wasn't shy about holding back. He was up and at it, ready for whatever come his way.

At least that's how Donny looked to be feeling until the bear woke back up.

* 3 *

IT WAS ENOUGH TO PISS OFF THE GOOD HUMOR MAN.

Here we were set out to build ourselves a little home-made revenge when God or Mother Nature decided to deal themselves in for a hand or two and fuck our expectations up like a herd of horny track men racing into a whorehouse on a Sudbury Saturday night.

Donny had one boot on the top of my shoulder blade and the other planted on the hood of the truck, looking for all the world like a reluctant surfer stepping up to ride the curl of a particularly dangerous wave, staring face-first into the muzzle of a pissed-off truck-slammed five hundred pound black bear.

I pushed on the door and rolled out of the truck like I thought I was in the middle of a Miami Vice episode. I don't rightly know what the hell I thought I was going to do, but all that I knew was I had to do it fast.

I couldn't see what Irvin was up to. Tyree was on the ground at the bear's feet, making a determined rolling wiggle towards the road. I wasn't worried about him. I was worried about Donny, who was just about to get his fool head chewed off.

I stepped up and shoved my hand, the same damn hand that Tyree had already stomped the hell out of, straight into the face of the bear, accidentally jamming my thumb into its eye socket. It didn't seem to see me coming, especially once my thumb was in its eye. It might have been that it was busy reaching out for Donny. It might be that the bear's peripheral vision had been somewhat fucked up by the collision with the truck. The possibilities were damn near endless but the amount of time in which I had to consider my options was pretty fucking nearly infinitesimal.

I leaned forward and jammed my thumb deeper into the bear's left eye, chocked my boot heel against the truck's front tire and braced myself hard, like I figured I was going to hold this bear at bay all by myself.

There's only one way to say this. A bear's head is freaking goddamn big. Even a Northern Ontario black bear can be a hell of a handful once you are stupid enough to get your hands wrapped around him. I could feel the bones in the black bear's face moving like fur-covered plate armour beneath my splayed open hand. So far I wasn't doing anything much more useful than pissing old Yogi off.

This one-handed Horatio-at-the-bridge Mexican bear stand-off had to be the one of the stupidest tricks I'd ever tried, and you have to keep in mind that this was coming from the fellow who once had roller skated through his high school prom with nothing on but a pair of Tinkerbelle wings and a camouflage of peppermint flavoured body paint. In about the time it took me to stick my thumb in and wiggle it around in the jelly-meat, I was certain that old bear was going to whirl about and rip my arm off and feed it back to me one knuckle at a time.

Bluntly put, I was fucked.

Only instead of ripping my arm off the bear stopped stock still and uttered out a roar that made Donny's Whitney Houston beagle call sound like a popcorn fart in the middle of a machine gun shoot-out in a Chinese gong factory. Mentioning a thunderstorm right about now would be just guilding the lily.

"Get the hell," I started to say, trying to yell at Donny to get the hell out of here, half expecting that big bruin bastard to toothpick my arm bone down to splintery forget-me-knuckles, when all of a sudden Irvin stepped up out of nowhere, quicker than you could say shit skidded skivvies, and slammed the business end of a genuine German Luger smack-square-dab into the side of the bear's skull and fired three shots off fast.

"Shit!"

I stepped back too slow, my thumb still jammed into the bear's left eye socket. My ears were ringing the Hallelujah Chorus with a Jimmy Page background of Hendrix-inspired guitar riffs. The side of my face was covered with what felt like bear brains. There were probably bits of the big old bastard's skull mixed in there with the shot-out bear brains, but I couldn't tell for sure. The whole world was ringing way too goddamn fast.

For a moment all I could do was stand there and stare at the bear's blown-out skull. The side of it was open wide enough for a red-headed woodpecker to build himself a comfortable nest. And then the damndest thing happened. I stood there staring and it looked like the bear was talking to me.

"Cover your tracks," the dead bear said. "Where ever you been ain't necessarily where ever you're going," Which at the time made about as much sense as a talking dead bear did.

"Only you can prevent forest fires," I answered back in a blurry bear-wrestling truck-wrecked brain-spattered kind of a daze.

Then I shook my head and looked again and the bear was deader than the disco duck and everything appeared natural. We were three guys and one convicted and duct taped arsonist, standing in the heart of the Northern Ontario woods over the body of a dead black bear. I expected we made an interesting tableau.

"Let go of that bear and stop messing around," Irvin said.

"Jesus Christ," I swore, dragging my hand clear of the poked-out eye socket. "You could have blown my hand off."

"I think I did," Irvin said.

I looked down at the hand.

Shit. He had. My thumb was half-missing. I could see a bit of the bone poked out like the stump of a broken pencil stub. The rest of the thumb looked like it had been run through an electronic pencil sharpener.

I tried to pinch the wound off, hoping to stop the bleeding, but I might as well try to stop traffic with a dirty look. Little spurts of blood shot out from the blasted thumb end. It felt like I was jerking off my thumb. I hope it respected me in the morning.

"Here," Irvin said, tearing a chunk from his t-shirt. "Wrap it in this."

"You shot my goddamn thumb off Irvin." I said while wrapping it in the t-shirt tear-off, trying hard not to wonder when the last time Irvin had washed this particular shirt was.

"You'll be okay," he told me.

"You shot my goddamned thumb off," I repeated. It was important to keep the facts straight.

"That's one less nail you'll have to clip," he offered. "Think of the money you'll save in manicures."

"It's my fucking thumb." I was losing it, and it was no wonder. You can hold an awful lot of pain in one hand, and nearly twice as much in one finger. That's how come hangnails hurt so badly.

"The bear would have done a whole lot worse," Irvin noted.

He had a point. I tried to grin around it, but the whiz-bang was wearing off, and I was starting to feel my thumb throbbing.

"Fuck," I said, scared and impressed at the same damned time. "We did it. You and I, we killed a bear with our bare hands."

"We didn't do it alone," Irvin said, pointing down at the dirt. "We did have ourselves a bit of help."

I looked down. There on the ground were Donny and Tyree. Tyree, bound hands and all, had both of his fists wrung white-knuckled around the bear's nuts, like a kid hanging onto a trick or treat bag. I figured that must have been what had distracted the bear just long enough for Irvin to get in there and administer his fistful of Luger lobotomy.

"Where the hell did that gun come from, anyway?" I asked.

"It was a World War 2 souvenir taken right off of an *SS Hauptsturmfuhrer*," Irvin said. "It was a gift from my grandfather. He brought it home from the war, along with a case of penicillin-resistant Belgian clap and a dirty French tattoo that looked a little like a turtle having sex with the pyramids of the Nile. I figured it might be handy to have along with me tonight, given the sort of work we were up to."

"Shit," I said. "All I got from my grandpa was this stupid assed name."

"Never mind the sorry state of your birthright," Irvin said. "Stop your yakking and get Donny the hell out of there."

That's when I looked down at Donny for the first time since Irvin had simultaneously shot the bear and my thumb off.

What the fuck?

It was around then that the bear brains that were splattered on the side of my skull started to itch as if they were crawling for my cowlick. It felt like they were trying to tell me something, but I didn't pay them any mind. I was stuck there, stock still, staring down at Donny. At first glance it looked like Donny was nuzzling the bear's tail, like he was trying to make a telephone call straight up through the bear's asshole.

Then I looked closer.

Donny's arm was jammed nearly elbow deep up the bear's tailpipe. He must have round-housed it in there fist first. I had to wonder at the nerve it must have took, dry-fisting a goddamn black bear square in the middle of a moonless night half-way through a one-handed shoot-out.

"That's who the hell you can thank for saving your life," Irvin pointed out.

"Holy crap," I said.

"And then some," Irvin said.

Donny just laid there, his face as white as a bucket of washed over bleach, making fresh-caught trout faces with his mouth.

It was as delicate situation as trying to extract a bushel of live cats from out of a bucket of dead porcupines. I reached my good hand down and caught hold of Donny's arm and helped him up from the dirt, while Irvin just stood there and snickered. I guess having a loaded pistol in your belt gave a fellow a certain sense of authority.

Donny's other arm came out of the bear's poop chute, with a cheek-flapping wet-fart sound. Donny's arm was covered in blood and some of the blackest and foulest crap I'd ever seen. It didn't smell one bit like lilies of the valley.

"Jesus Christ, Donny," I said. "You must have had your arm worked right up into that there bear's lower colon."

Donny made a few more fish faces. He was shivering in spite of the fact that it was August-hot and sticky out here.

"Get up here, Donny," I said, leaning back and putting my weight into it. He stood shakily, like a house of cards just waiting to be blown down. He held his poop stained arm off to one side, like he might have wanted to yank it out of its socket and throw it away on the compost heap. All the same, he was hanging onto something that might have been a piece of bear crap, or maybe the bear's pancreas.

"I got it," Donny said. He was still shaking, his bones poured from rubber earthquakes and slinky wire.

"What do you got Donny?" I asked slowly.

Donny looked up at me just as slowly, like he'd just done the single biggest thing in the world, and I guess he had.

"I got hold of the bear's soul," he said, holding the fistful out towards me.

I didn't want to look at whatever he was holding. It was small and it seemed to be moving.

"It's his soul," Donny explained. "As long as I got it he ain't going anywhere."

Having woken up in my share of ugly married women's beds I knew damn well what shock could do to a man, so I phrased my next words carefully.

"You did good Donny," I told him.

"I ain't letting go," he said, pushing the piece of bear at my face.

I made a few fresh-caught trout mouths of my own, and then he smiled that Donny smile of his again and I figured everything was going to be okay, sooner or later.

"I'm holding it tight," Donny said. "There's got to be some kind of sacrifice."

He wasn't making much sense, but how much sense could I expect after what we'd been through. I decided that he'd be okay, although I wasn't all that sure about myself.

"We got to eat it," Donny said.

"Hunh?"

"We got to eat the bear," Donny said. "You can't kill something wild for no reason. It's a sin."

I was about to point out that self-preservation counts high among my reasons for bear slaughter, when Irvin spoke up.

"He's right," Irvin said. "We got to eat some of it."

He knelt down with his hunting knife in his hands, already hacking into the hide and cutting loose a chunk of meat. "We don't have to eat it all. Just a bit will do."

"Irvin, are you completely fucked in the head, or just generally soft?"

Irvin stared at me, his eyes as hard and deep as the twin barrels of a shotgun.

"We got to eat some of the meat," he repeated. "And then we got to apologise for killing it. Billy Three-Legs Tootoosis is a hell of a lot smarter than he looks."

He threw me his Zippo.

I caught it in my left hand.

"Start a fire," Irvin said. "But careful, mind you, we don't want to be setting the whole damned place ablaze."

I gathered a bit of kindling.

And then I lit a fire.

* 4 *

WELL I WOULDN'T EXACTLY CALL IT HOT CUISINE. The fact was it wasn't even close to tepid. We didn't have enough time to build ourselves a proper bed of coals, so we settled for charring it over the open flames. We held it off to one side so that the bear fat wouldn't flare up in the flames, turning it rotisserie style to keep the juices from running off of it and drying it out.

I am certain we picked up enough pestilence and corruption to single-handedly bring about the rebirth of the Bubonic Plague, but we got her down and said our apologies and made things right with the Great Spirit or whoever the hell was watching from up there above the pines.

"Well, that sure hit the spot," Irvin said.

"Would that be the spot of indigestion or that spot of pneumatic botulism that is germinating somewhere southwest of my lower intestine?" I asked.

"Quit your belly aching," Irvin chided me. "Let's get this asshole under way."

He pointed at Tyree.

Only I got to wondering about Tyree. The fact was, I'd be wondering all of the way through the bear meat.

What Tyree had done hadn't been all that much compared to arm-fucking a full grown black bear, but who was to say that bear hadn't been held back just enough on account of Tyree hanging on so tightly to Fozzie's funky fuzzy teabags. Who was to say that Tyree hadn't just saved my life, as much as Irvin kept telling me it was Donny who'd done the deed?

"Get that thought out of your head right now," Irvin warned me like he could read my mind. "He didn't save you. Donny did."

I stared at Irvin. He always had a touch of magic and secrecy about him, what with his making guns appear and seeing in the dark and knowing the proper apologies to make to a dead bear.

All the same, I had to argue with him this time.

"Are you sure about that?" I asked.

"I said it, didn't I?"

Irvin wasn't known for much exaggeration. The man had all of the imagination of petrified dog turd.

"So what's your verdict, your honor?" I asked, pointing down at Tyree. "What the hell do you figure we ought to do with him for now?"

Irvin looked over at me as if I'd just said the stupidest thing since tri-party politics.

"What the fuck else do you figure we're going to do?" Irvin said. "The same thing we came out here to do in the first place."

Irvin hawked up a jumbo-sized loogie and let it gravitationally anoint itself down onto the top of Tyree's head. It hit home with a soft wet plop that sounded like it would stay stuck for a hell of a long time.

"We're going to kill the little fucker, that's what we're going to do."

* 5 *

WE DARKED THE LIGHTS ON THE TRUCK and left it where it was, hoping that the engine would start when we got back. We'd borrowed the truck from the freight yard, and would have to get it back by morning, but if we had to leave it here we'd probably be safe enough. These trucks went missing all the time, and like it as not they'd just blame it on Tyree and call it a day.

"What the hell kind of name is Tyree, anyway?" Irvin asked.

"How the fuck should I know?" I asked. "Maybe he made it up."

"Who in the hell would make up their own name?"

I was thinking about my own name, and how I planned to change it.

"A lot of people change their names," I said. "Folks are re-inventing themselves all of the time."

"Don't fix nothing if it isn't broke," Irvin said. "What do you think, Donny?"

"I wonder if there are any more bears out here." Donny wondered aloud.

It was a good question, given all that had happened.

"If there ARE any more bears out there Donny, you can syrup them up with your sweet talking before up and fist-fucking them to death," Irvin said.

I glowered at Irvin's back. The man had all the sensitivity of a sandblast enema.

"There ain't nothing out here but trees and rocks and the dark, and a whole lot of fucking mosquitoes," I said, trying to cheer Donny up.

"What's over them hills, do you figure?" He asked.

"More hills," Irvin said. "Let's get moving."

We followed the railroad tracks, straight on out into the darkness of the night. I did my best to stay downwind of Donny. The bear stink on him was beginning to fulminate. We both were stinking of bear, shit, fear and genuine funk. I heard there were folks in Korea who would pay an awful lot for a bear's gall bladder. I figured between what Donny was wearing on his arm and the halo of minced bear head cheese I was wearing on my forehead we ought to have both been worth a small fortune on E-bay.

We kept on walking, one step after another.

About that time the bear brains started talking to me, good and loud.

* 6 *

NOW TALKING IS A GOOD THING. It's how we fill in the gaps between what needs doing, what wants doing, and whatever the hell we're dreaming about doing when we stare up at the ceiling before falling into sleep.

Talk is a kind of glue that holds lives together. It's not the work that you do that makes the engineer such a good buddy to the guy working in the caboose. It's the stories that you tell over a beer or a coffee or a campfire that makes a man's memories loom out loud and long.

So maybe that's what this bear was doing, trying to talk to me. Maybe he was trying to get to know what it was like to have thumbs and worry about something else besides making a few more cubs and fattening that belly that needed filling by winter. Maybe he was just trying to understand the simple asshole that had left the tip of his thumb buried in the humorous jelly of his left eye socket, just an inch or two shy of his Jasper-Jellystone dreaming frontal lobe.

Or maybe he was just fucking around in whatever roomy dark cave of an afterlife Northern Ontario black bears inhabit after they been Lugered to death.

"The path is long," the spirit of the bear said to me. "And it touches all sides."

"No kidding," I said. "You ought to try walking it while you're dragging a duct taped arsonist in tow."

"Whiner," The dead bear said.

"Winnie," I retorted.

Repartee is my middle name.

You get a lot of practice up here in Northern Ontario, in between the crib and the curling and listening to the diesels hoot down the line. Life up here has its own kind of rhythm, hard and driving like a train engine, and then there's them long stretches of quiet in between, and it hardly surprises a fellow when he can find himself the time to converse with the dead spirit of a black bear.

"Should I apologize again?" I asked. "I know the Cree are big about apologizing to the animals they catch and kill. It wasn't really me that killed you. You know that, don't you? I'm just the guy who fondled your left eye socket up close and personal. In some cultures that's often considered a kind of pre-emptive mating strike."

"That's okay," The spirit of the bear said. "Shit happens, every day. It all gets washed away in the flush of life."

"Hakuna Matata," I agreed. "What goes around comes around."

"The past is nothing more than a canvas for what's going on right now," The bear expounded. The spirit of the bear was making a surprising amount of sense, given that he was dead and all. Maybe that gave him a little sense of perspective.

"Dead men walk the tracks," The dead bear said.

I looked over at the rails, and all at once I could see the spirits of the dead men walking, the navvies and the chinks and the road gangs who'd laid down the steel and the timber like a stitch sewn out across a giant forever carcass.

"But they tell no tales," I answered.

"They tell no tales but they sure as hell leave trails," The dead bear said.

"You're bound and determined to get the last word in, ain't you?" I said.

In the chat-room of my inner child imagination I stared into the dead bear's eyes. They seemed like black holes, sucking me downward. I could see something swimming up towards me in the dark sea of the dead bear's eyes. It looked a little like Irvin.

"Earth to Hanny, Earth to Hanny, Houston we have got a fucking problem."

"Huh?" I looked around. The bear was gone. Irvin was staring at me like I was a bug under a microscope. Only something was changed. Irvin was wearing a robe of bear fur and black feathers that looked like it might have been growing out of his skin.

"You were sleepwalking," He said. "And you were talking to yourself."

"Daydreaming, I guess," I said.

"Not dreaming," Irvin corrected. "You've been walking wide. That's a danger in the dark places of the North woods. There are shadows out here cast by no tree or rock. Dark places where you can step through into another plane of existence."

I looked up at Irvin, and I could see it wasn't really Irvin.

"I must still be dreaming," I said. "You're Irvin, only not Irvin."

"Not dreaming. You've been walking wide. There's a big difference," Irvin-not-Irvin said. "The world used to be a dark colorless plain of nothingness. There weren't any people or plants or animals. There weren't any mountains, lakes or forests. There was nothing but nothingness. Then the spirit awoke from the shadows and stood up and began rooting around in the darkness looking for food or drink."

He took a breath.

Spit.

And then kept on talking.

"He turned up mountains, and pissed down rivers, and the dreams he planted grew up into people and animals and birds and life," Irvin-not-Irvin went on. "Then they all started moving around in the darkness, stirring up the wind and calling down the rain and drawing out the moon, and the fire that burned in their collective hearts grew out to become the sun."

"I have no fucking idea what you are talking about," I said to Irvin-not-Irvin.

Irvin-not-Irvin smiled. His smile looked a little like Donny's, crooked at one side like his happiness was leaking out.

"Sure you do," Irvin-not-Irvin said. "We all know it when we go dreaming, when we go walking wide. We're all part of this world and when we touch it there are ripples that sing out and touch everything else. Man, woman, moose and bear. We're all a part of this big wide walking, reaching out in every direction, touching everywhere and everything all at once."

Then Irvin-not-Irvin winked, and in his wink I saw the great one-eyed bear, with my own thumbprint still burning somewhere deep inside that black hole eye socket.

Irvin-not-Irvin smiled one more time, that half-cracked Donny smile of his that he'd borrowed or maybe owned in the first place.

"Wake up," Irvin-not-Irvin said, and I did.

* 7 *

"SHIT," I SAID, STARTING MY EYES WIDE OPEN.

"Wake up," Irvin said. "You're asleep at the switch and we got work to do."

"Shit, shit," I repeated.

"You're covered in it. So is Donny," Irvin pointed out. That happens sometimes. We still got work to do. Stop talking to yourself and let's get to it."

I hadn't been talking to myself, and I knew that for a fact, but I wasn't about to argue the point with Irvin.

"Sorry," I said, because it seemed simpler than trying to explain what I'd just been through. Simpler, on account of I wasn't all that sure myself what I'd just been through.

"I'm awake now Irvin," I assured him.

He grunted, like he wasn't all that certain if I was or not.

"You've been talking to the bear, haven't you?" Irvin asked.

I looked back at Irvin, double checking to make sure I wasn't still dreaming.

"How the fuck did you know?" I asked him.

"Who else is out here to talk to?" Irvin said, like it made all of the sense in the world. "Now come on. It's been a long night, but we've still got a long way to go."

It turned out to be a whole lot longer than the three of us could have ever guessed.

* 8 *

WE WERE ABOUT FIVE MILES OUT from town and my feet were channelling the bunions of the collective casualties of the Trail of Tears and the Bataan Death March. We were far enough down the line that it wasn't likely there'd be any switchman humping boxcars down this way and accidentally disturbing us before we were finished.

Finished. That was one hell of a word. How do you tie up a knot like this one? I knew where this was all going to end but I don't know how in hell we ever figured it was going to be anywhere close to be being finished.

"Do we have to do this?" I asked Irvin.

"What kind of a question is that?" Irvin asked back. "The bastard burned a couple of your buddies to death and killed my big brother. He sent them up in flames like last year's gas bill. What the hell else can we do?"

"You're sure about that are you?" Tyree asked. "You figure I did all that you think I did?"

We all jumped like flung-bungeed cats. These were the first words Tyree had said all night, since we'd jumped him outside of the Legion Hall and tied him up and gagged him. He hadn't even said anything after he'd chewed the duct tape gag loose. Maybe he figured on saving his breath for his death song.

Personally, I didn't understand this kind of thinking. If I was walking my last mile and knew it, I don't believe I'd shut up for a minute. I'd talk a steel blue streak, trying to make up for everything I wasn't going to be able to say later. There are a whole lot of things I haven't had a chance to say yet.

Then there were all of those things I missed the chance to say. Things that I wished I had the chance to say, even now. I wished I could go back and tell Beth Skinner how hot she had looked in her cinnamon and lemonade striped cheerleading outfit, back before Marie and I said "I do" to each other. I wished I had told my high school track instructor what a colossal aneurism he'd been for taking me off of the track team just as I was getting fast enough to break the school record in the 100 yard dash just because I'd gone and chucked our champion javelin chucker straight through three lockers full of soccer balls, for having the nerve to look sideways at my girlfriend's ass. I wished I'd had the chance to tell the javelin chucker how sorry I was that there hadn't been a fourth locker.

And more than anything I wished that I'd found the time to tell my dad how much I looked up to him, back before I found myself staring down at him laying there in that long dark box.

If I closed my eyes now I knew I would see him staring up at me out of the darkness, his face as cold and hard as that last chunk of frozen purple meat at the bottom of the deep freeze. I knew he would open his mouth and he would say something to me in the voice of the bear that I just didn't think I wanted to hear right now.

So I kept my eyes open and promised myself I wouldn't blink.

"I think we ought to let him talk," I said.

"Who, Donny?"

"No, Tyree."

"What for?" Irvin asked. "That'd be just a waste of good air, if you ask me. Haven't you heard there's an ozone crisis going on? Keep yakking like you are, using up all of that good atmosphere, and the next thing you know we are ALL going to need to wipe our assholes with SPF 75 sunscreen."

"Donny's bean-farts do just as much damage to the ozone layer," I pointed out. "Besides, I think Tyree deserves a say in this."

"He's had his say. He said it when the first flames went up. He said it when my brother's face started to split open from the heat, all sizzling like bear meat grilling down on the barbecue."

"I think Hanny is right," Donny said. "We all ought to have a say."

"Sure you all ought to," Irvin said. He whirled back around, back-handing Donny so hard that one of his teeth spit out. "What do you have to say to that, fuckhead?"

Donny hit the ground. His mouth was bleeding.

"I think he chipped my toof," Donny said.

He tried to grin, but it was all lopsided and wrong. That Donny smile didn't quite look the same. Something had been twisted in it and I didn't think it could ever be fixed.

I looked at Irvin, hard as I could.

"You didn't have to do that Irvin," I said.

"Didn't not have to do it either," Irvin said right back at me. "Now shut the fuck up. We're here."

Sure enough we were, right at Five mile switch, out amongst the tall jack pines. You could see the signs of the old bushfire if you knew what to look for. It had taken out the woods for miles. Everybody figured it for a heat lightning strike. Donny and I had been out here blueberry picking. We caught shit for wandering so damn far off the track.

Now there was nothing but jack pines and more blueberries. The pines always came back after the fire rolled through. There was something in the heat that popped their seeds from the pine cones. The blueberries grew thicker than usual here as well. I guess ashes were great for fertilizer.

There was nothing else out here, but the switch.

And us.

Irvin looked down at his glow-in-the-dark wristwatch.

"We got eight minutes," He said. "Let's get to it."

I did my best to let Tyree down gently onto the track, but Irvin shoved me and him down as hard as he could.

"Asshole," Irvin said. "You fellows couldn't tie your shoes together without a detailed set of paint-by-number instructions. Stop dicking around and get his hand jammed down into that switch."

A railroad switch is a pretty simple device, designed to join two ends of track together, when a train is leaving one track and traveling onto another. Basically, there's a big swing bar of steel that levers back and forth. The train follows the swing bar, either straight on, or onto another track. There's a gap in between the swing bar and the rail that closes tight when the swing bar moves. A fellow had best be careful about where he sets his boot when he's crossing the tracks. If he gets his foot jammed in a swinging switch, he's apt to bust an ankle, or worse.

"This is sure going to hurt," Donny said.

"No worse than proctologically poking your arm up a bear's butt," Irvin pointed out. "This bastard deserves it."

Donny and I just stared at each other. We'd been beat and broken and damn near bear-bitten. The fact was we were just too tired and broke down to argue the point. We'd do whatever Irvin told us to.

Soldiers get that way in battle. The sergeant says get up over that hill and face down the machine gun, and up over the hill they go. It works the same way on section gangs and track crews. Whatever the foreman says, sooner or later goes.

Donny and I forced Tyree's left hand down into the switch, between the swinging bar and the rail. The switch was set electronically and a computer timing device three hundred miles away would shift the switch over, bringing the two pieces of metal together, so that the CPR train could successfully switch onto the CNR track.

By Irvin's watch this entire process would take place in about six minutes time.

Tyree tried to kick free, but the two of us had a firm grip on him now. There didn't seem to be much fight left in him. I guess he was tired too.

"Tyree," Irvin said. "You've been found guilty of setting a match and gasoline to the Hammer Abbey Railroad Hotel and smoking six men to death, as well as Henry Tompkins, the night clerk, and a perfectly good tomcat named One-Eye. One of those men was my brother, Gilbert. For burning him and those six other fellows, you're going to have to die."

Tyree just lay there and stared up at the three of us. That made it worse. It might have been easy if he'd kept on fighting. That would have given us something to do while we were holding his hand down, waiting for the switch to swing shut.

"You got anything to say in your defense?"

"What the fuck good would it do if I did?" Tyree asked. "I've got nothing to say that you want to hear."

"Irvin, I don't think he did it," Donny said.

"What?" Irvin asked.

"I said I don't think he did it."

Irvin stared at Donny. I could feel the strength of his gaze even in the darkness, shining out at us like the blind beam of a flashlight.

"You got something to say?"

"I don't think he did it," Donny repeated for the third time.

"Donny, I truly like you," Irvin said. "You're a good boy, and there's damn few men would have jammed their arm where you did, but sometimes you act dumb enough to dig fence postholes in a snow bank."

Donny opened his mouth to speak, and the switch closed shut. I was holding Tyree's arm at the wrist when the steel closed. I felt the chill of the cold steel rail kiss the side of my pinkie and the sensation damn near leaped up and burned me. It didn't make much of a noise coming together on Tyree's hand, just a sort of a crackling quiet like someone crumpling up a potato chip bag in the dark.

Tyree yelled loud enough to out-deafen those three bear-killing Luger shots and Donny's beagle-humping Whitney Houston serenade. He screamed all of the breath out of his lungs, and a few molecules of oxygen that he'd sucked in from his mama's umbilical, back when he was floating around in her belly-tank. The scream lasted a good minute, and then bled off to a rasping sort of sigh. All the color left Tyree's face and ran out onto the dirt of the trackside. I could see Tyree's face pale and glowing, like he'd grown a moon atop his shoulders and then everything went calm.

Tyree lay there staring up at me. I wondered if he was bleeding or if maybe the switch had closed tightly enough to cut off his arterial flow. I wondered about the band-aid qualities of a CNR rail, not having much faith in a cauterization by steel. I had the feeling that maybe the metal was drinking Tyree's blood. I could picture that, the blood flowing through the steel rail, like a fat rusty vein running right across this continent. All of the men who'd given their lives to building this rail line, one dead man for every foot of steel some folks said, their blood was still pumping in the piston of the diesel and the scream of the train.

I saw the bear looking one-eyed out from both of Tyree's eyes. It was trying to tell me something and for the life of me I couldn't understand what.

"He's as guilty as Iscariott," Irvin pronounced. "And now he's fucked."

Irvin looked down at his wristwatch. I saw his face shining in the soft electronic glow.

"How much time?" I asked.

"That train will be here in five minutes," Irvin said. "The switch will hold him fast enough until the train rolls out the guilt in him. When that comes we'd best make ourselves scarce."

I stood up, half expecting Tyree to start kicking, but all of the fight had gone out of him. He lay there on the tracks with his left hand vanished between those two bars of iron rail like it had been cut clean off. He kind of looked a little like Donny, with his arm jammed inside the bear's pooper.

"The train will roll over him, the switch will click back, and they'll think he was out here drinking." Irvin said. "Some folks will say accident and others will whisper suicide and everybody will privately figure that Tyree finally got just what was coming to him.

"What if they CSI his body?" Donny asked. "We got our fingerprints all over him."

"You watch too damn much television," Irvin said. "This is the town police we're talking about. On the first account there won't be any body left, once that train rolls over it. They'll be picking Tyree up in a bushel basket, assuming the bears and raccoons and crows don't get him, assuming there are any bears left after Daniel bear-fucker Boone here gets done with fist-fucking them all to death."

Irvin kept on hammering on that bear-fucking crack. I figured it had to hurt, but Donny didn't say anything. He just stood there, hanging onto whatever he'd dragged out of that bear, looking down at Tyree.

I placed the sole of my boot flat out onto the rail. I felt the vibration of the distant train, humming through the steel. It was coming soon.

"Can you feel it coming?" Irvin asked.

I nodded.

Tyree just lay there.

"Right on time," Irvin nodded. He was pleased with how it was all going down, like he'd finished a job on schedule.

"Irvin," Donny said. "He didn't do it."

"What?"

"I'm telling you he didn't do it."

I could hear the train in the distance now. I could hear something even stronger in Donny's voice.

"How do you know he didn't?" Irvin asked, laying his words out slow.

"I just know."

I could see the light in the distance, the headlamp shining out like a long bright knife into the wooded darkness. I bet you God sees the world that way, with one good eye staring out into the lying shadows.

"I just know," Donny repeated, and that's all I let him get out. The train was close enough to see us, if we didn't move fast.

"Jump," I shouted, catching the two of them by their necks and pushing us all three down into the darkness of the surrounding bushes as the train rolled on by.

We lay there in the darkness listen to the chunk-chunk-chunk as the cars rolled over the track.

"Stay down," I whispered to Donny.

Right about then I was telling him a whole lot more than just stay down in the dirt. I was begging him to keep whatever he wanted to say to himself. We'd just killed Tyree. He needed to die, on account of Irvin said so. I couldn't live with any other kind of reality, right now.

That train was coming fast. I could hear it in the distance, even smell it coming, singing out in the hum of the steel rail, and the chunking sound as it rolled over each hard-buried iron spike. I heard the roar of the bear mauling through the thunder of the diesel and the steel.

And then it was on us. The train rolled and roared past, and then it was thunder all around us, the steady chunk-chunk-chunk sound as each truck wheel rolled over the properly closed switch.

I thought about Tyree, under those wheels. There was no way he could have escaped. I wondered how long he'd feel the steel rolling across each nerve. How long does a memory scream?

I pictured him caught up underneath the steel wheels, dragged and broken and torn and flung. I kept expecting to hear a scream. I don't know how I'd figure

I'd hear it over the hungry roar of the train. Death would travel far faster than any scream could ever hope to run. Tyree's throat would be torn out and pulped, and the memory of last night's song in the shower and the "Get fucked," he'd thrown at a co-worker and the half-assed joke he'd cracked to the cute Tim Horton's waitress would all be flattened out onto the steel rails, to couple with the lonely working dreams of all of the navvies and the chinks and the working men who had died laying these tracks down across our wide impassive country over the last century making a scar that wouldn't stick.

If a scream had worked its way up through Tyree's trachea and harped through the plucking vocal chords it would have been whisked away in the slipstream of the rushing steel wheels.

I couldn't deal with that thought. I pushed my face down into the dirt and the dead pine needles, smelling the ash of the long forgotten bushfire hiding deep in the dirt, a last track and trace of that long ago fire and in the silence of the roaring steel tracks behind me I heard Donny saying over and over to Irvin, "He didn't do it, he didn't do it." in tune with the song of the rail and I wondered who did.

There was only one way to find out.

I rolled over and I caught Donny in a neck hold. I had grown up watching Yvon Carpentier and Killer Kowalski and Mad Dog Vachon going at it in the Grand Prix wrestling ring. I knew the flying mare and the arm bar and the incapacitating eye gouge.

Come down to it, I could even fake a pretty good drop kick, although it usually resulted in inflicting more injury upon me than upon the inflictee.

The only problem with this reasoning was that Donny had watched all of those matches with me, and he knew just as many tricks. He eeled out of my neck hold and pistoned an elbow back into the side of my head. I felt that elbow greasing off of the bear brains, and I wondered if the black bear's brains would have anything to say to Donny's elbow bone.

We rolled up against the roots of a jack pine and Donny pulled loose and kicked back at me. I felt Donny's mule-kicking work boots working over my ribs, and I reached up blindly past his boot and followed the trail of denim up to the crotch. I caught hold of what counted and I squeezed.

Tyree had taught me a trick or two, too.

Donny howled like a gut shot wolf, making a face that only a necropheliac could love, sucking in his cheeks and owling out his eyes and rolling them back until I was certain he was staring directly at his long lost childhood memories. I kept on squeezing, going for broke.

"Who did it, Donny?" I asked, hanging onto his denimed testicles. "Who burned the hotel down?"

"I didn't mean to," Donny said, weeping real tears. "I didn't mean to start the fire."

"What?" I asked.

He was crying, the snot rolling and slithering out of his nose, the sobs hitching along like boxcars loaded full of guilt.

"I didn't mean to start the fire," Donny repeated.

And then Irvin was on him, throwing me aside like I was a discarded beer can, catching hold of Donny by the throat and shaking him like he expected a money back refund.

"What'd you say?" Irvin asked. "What the fuck did you say?"

Donny was back to making those trout faces again. Irvin kept throttling and shaking him, not letting up for a minute, looking for an answer but not letting one escape.

"What'd you say?" Irvin repeated.

I tried to catch hold of Irvin and pull him off of Donny, but I would have had better luck trying to pull an unshot-up black bear from off of a honey-packed beehive. Irvin was tensed steel, shot through with a white hot line of blue lightning, strung with hatred and an undeniable need for vengeance.

"What the fuck did you say?"

By now his voice was so hoarse I could hear the bear growling in his throat, like it had climbed down inside of him and taken over his existence.

Donny didn't stand a chance. Irvin had his hands around Donny's throat and was squeezing the breath out of him. It takes a lot to kill a man by bare-handed strangulation. It isn't as easy as they show on the television. There's muscle in your neck and your shoulders, especially when you've worked for a living like we had.

Still, Donny wasn't looking that good. Irvin was pretty determined to get his fair share of mayhem in. If assault and battery were a pinball game Irvin had just racked up a score that tallied way past the free game mark.

I tried wrapping my arms around Irvin's waist, hoping to bear-hug him away from Donny. That didn't work nearly as well as it did on television either. Big John of the roller derby Thunderbirds always made it look damn easy, but I might as well have been trying to throttle an oak tree.

"Irvin," I tried shouting at him. "He didn't fucking do it, Irvin."

But Irvin wasn't listening.

I kept reaching around, and then I felt the butt of the Luger. I drew it out of Irvin's belt and jammed it into his ear canal as hard as I could.

"If you don't let go of him, Irvin," I said, shouting loud enough for him to hear me through the pistol barrel. "I'm going to have to blow your skull out."

I didn't know how to cock the fucking gun, so I settled for making a click sound with my tongue and teeth, hoping I sounded dangerous.

He seemed to hear that click loud and clear or maybe the barrel was talking through the grip of my fist.

I'd never fired a Luger before. I'd only seen them in World War II movies. I hadn't fired any hand guns at all, now that I thought of it. The closest I'd come was my six-shooter Lone Ranger cap gun when I was a kid, and even that misfired as often as not. I had absolutely no way of knowing if the Luger would go off in my hands or not. I didn't know if I wanted to shoot Irvin, even by accident. I didn't know anything for certain.

Donny kept opening his mouth and closing it, catching a few random mosquitoes in the process. That wasn't doing any good to anyone as far as I could see.

"For Christ sake, Donny, say something."

He opened and closed his mouth one more time before finding a half a dozen useless words.

"I didn't mean to do it," Donny croaked.

I felt Irvin tense, like he was going to jump. I screwed the barrel a little tighter into his ear canal, breaking some of the soft pucker flesh. I hoped it was intimidating him, but he didn't look all that intimidated to me. I might as well have been squeegeeing a pussy willow Q-tip in his ear for all of the good it seemed to be doing me.

"Say something besides that, Donny," I begged. "Say something he'll listen to."

Donny started talking. "The woods. I was blueberry picking and burning ants with my magnifying glass. I didn't mean to start a fire. I didn't mean to burn it all down."

Holy Christ.

Donny wasn't talking about the hotel fire, he was talking about the bush fire, way back when we were kids. He'd reached back into his memory and dredged up the ancient past.

"For shit's sake, Donny, that was years ago," I said. "What about the hotel fire?"

"Huh?" Donny asked.

It was good to have a vocabulary. I tried to put it to better use than I had so far, but Irvin beat me to the punch.

"You mean you didn't start the Railroad Hotel fire?" Irvin asked.

"I burned down all the trees," Donny said. "I didn't mean to. I was just playing."

"But what about the hotel?" Irvin kept on digging.

"He didn't do it, Irvin." I said. "It was a misunderstanding. He's talking about burning down Jack Pine Stretch, for Christ sake. We only guessed he was talking about the hotel."

Irvin looked like the lights were going in his brain, one by one.

"We were guessing, do you get it? We were guessing about Donny and we were guessing about Tyree. We were wrong about Donny. That means maybe we were wrong about Tyree too."

It took a lot to get through to Irvin.

"Could be," He said.

I kept working at it.

"Focus, Donny. We are here for the hotel fire," I said. "How did it get started?"

"I don't know how it happened," Donny said. "I just don't know."

"Do you see?" I asked Irvin.

Irvin kept looking like he was chewing over it. I figured I'd better be safe.

"I'm keeping this," I said, pointing the Luger straight at Irvin. "I don't know if I'm going to use it or not. Don't fuck me with me Irvin. I'm just not in the mood for it right now."

"So what the hell are we going to do?" He asked.

"Same thing we set out to do," I said. "We're going up to that switch and we're going to scrape up whatever is left of Tyree and we're going to bury it. Isn't that right, Donny?"

Donny looked agreeable. If he'd had a tail he would have wagged it.

Irvin didn't look half so happy. He looked as if he'd love to tell me to go fuck a splintery knothole, just as soon as I let go of the Luger.

So I hung onto the Luger.

We walked up to the tracks; only by the time we got there Tyree was long gone.

* 9 *

IT'S EASY TO LOSE THINGS. You can lose your car in a parking lot if you're not careful how much you drink at the party you were driving to. You can lose the remote beneath the couch cushions if you're not careful with how much you eat between commercials. You can lose your girlfriend and your wife, sometimes even at the same time. You can lose your dog, hell, you can even lose your mind if you think too hard about it, but losing a body is something else entirely.

The switch was still there. It had opened, now that the train had passed. The signal station, three hundred miles away, had automatically closed the circuit and opened the switch.

There was something clumped in the metal where the switch had closed and reopened. It looked like a bit of crushed meat. Actually to me it looked an awful lot like the smoked meat slices you get in a those plastic boil-a-bags, only with a lot more ketchup.

I didn't want to look any closer.

"Well you got to hand it to Tyree," Irvin said. "He sure knows how to make his mark."

That did it. I shoved Irvin hard. While he was catching his footing I clocked him with the butt of the Luger, getting a good swing on it and putting my weight behind all of it. The Luger might have gone off, I suppose, but right about then I was pissed.

Irvin went down on one knee. I pointed the Luger and cocked it like a pro as if my hands suddenly knew what they had to do. I felt the spirit of a German SS Hauptsturmführer moving through my arm, hungry for a revenge-by-proxy on the verdammt Allies who had stormed over his homeland and eaten all of his bratwurst and sauerkraut.

I stared at Irvin. There was blood leaking from his scalp, but he didn't seem to mind that. He was staring just as hard as me. Something had changed between us. Right then and there I knew that whatever else went on tonight that Irvin and I just weren't ever going to look at each other the same way we used to.

"You want me and Donny to look away for a minute or two while you try real hard to go and fuck yourself, Irvin?" I asked, only this time I meant it.

Irvin kept staring at me, like he was committing every detail of me to memory. I kept the gun pointed straight at him, just in case he took it in his head to take a swing at me. Luger or not, Irvin was still nobody I wanted to fuck around with. Even on a good day he was a bad man.

"Where'd Tyree go?" Donny asked.

"Either that switch took his hand off at the wrist, or the train did," Irvin said. "It looks to me like he crawled that way."

"Maybe he yanked himself free," Donny said. "That switch closed on his hand awful hard."

I tried to picture that. Tried to wrap my head around the kind of desperation it would take to rip your own hand off.

"Maybe the train ripped it off," Irvin repeated like he was trying to talk himself into it. "It looks like he crawled that way."

He pointed to the left of the track. I looked where he was pointing, turning the gun. He could have jumped me then, I suppose, but the two of us were busy staring at a path of blood glinting in the starlight.

There is always a trail if you look hard enough for something to follow along with.

* 11 *

TYREE MUST HAVE CRAWLED A LONG WAY INTO THE DARKNESS. Irvin, Donny and I had followed the blood trail for a good twenty minutes, stalking him down like a wounded deer but there was still no sign of him but the long drag of burnt vermillion.

We kept at it. I wouldn't stand for anything else. We had to put this thing to a finish.

"There's no way he could have crawled this far," Irvin said. "We've missed him for sure."

"There's no way to know that for sure," I said. "You're just guessing."

"There's a lot of that going around." Irvin said.

Donny didn't say a thing. He just kept walking along with us, occasionally gingering his fingertips across his jaw line, right about where Irvin had hit him. Funny, how that was. You face a truck wreck, hand wrestle a bear to death, stage an execution and it's your best buddy who really leaves the mark.

I felt the dirt and debris crushing beneath my feet. Every step we took out here killed something. A leaf, a bug, a fern, it was all fair game. We stomped it all down flat, like a steamroller road crew from hell.

Nobody said a word. We just kept walking into the darkness, three not-so-wise-men stumbling through the black of the forest hunting down a trail of blood. I might as well have been a shadow of Irvin, him walking in front of me and me following blindly behind pointing the gun so that I felt in command of the whole situation. Donny trailed the two of us like a lag-along echo-ghost.

How far had Tyree crawled? Why hadn't he bled out yet? There's a hell of a lot of plumbing and pipe work in your average wrist. How much blood was there in one man?

I didn't know. I was only guessing.

The trail kept snailing out in front of us like a taunt. I wondered if somebody might not have been dragging him. That was possible. Might be it was just one of the track crew, or just some wandering woodsman who happened to be out for a two a.m. stroll through a moonless wooded stretch of jack pines. Might be it was a bum or a really big family of raccoons. Might be they'd found what was left of Tyree and were dragging him home for a game of one-handed crib. Stranger things had happened.

The mosquitoes were thick around us, their buzzing a constant hum, like power moving through the darkness, whirling nits of electrons swinging around some dark atom of guilt. I could hear something following us in the darkness in the woods beyond my sight. I could hear it pushing the branches aside and parting the shadows and snuffling through the underbrush. Whatever it was it sounded god-awful big. Maybe the bear had a buddy, only this sounded bigger than a bear. Bigger even than a moose.

Fuck. I was losing it. I needed some sleep. I needed a drink.

I needed to finish this.

I hung harder onto the Luger, welding my fingerprints into its machine-tooled grip. I told myself I could take care of everything. The memory of the SS trooper assured me that it was all right to just simply follow orders. I damned near believed it.

And then we found Tyree.

He was crawling through the woods, hauling himself along through the brackle and the underbrush, using his one good arm like he was attempting to swim the sidestroke through the dirt. His hand was completely torn off and he looked like he'd lost a hell of a lot more blood then he should have had in him in the first place.

"Holy fuck," Donny swore.

Irvin giggled. Right then and there I would have cheerfully shot the son of a bitch, except there was something hiding out beyond the darkness and the silence that I didn't want to wait for all by myself. I didn't think Donny or Tyree were going to be much of a help if whatever that was decided to come out of the darkness. Irvin, bastard or not, was a tough fuck-nut and I wanted him handy if something went down.

I knelt down beside Tyree, like I was kneeling beside a cocked-open bear trap. I could feel some kind of dark energy emanating from him, like the humming you feel in your bones if you stand too close to a power generator.

"You're okay," I said. "We're here."

I don't know how comforting that particular sentiment was, considering that we were the three assholes who had put him in this predicament in the first place but I just had to say something.

"I can't find my hand," Tyree said. His voice sounded like something inside of it had broken, like glass and those little tin ringer-thingy bells that you see on tricycles and little kid's bikes. "I've lost it somewhere."

I hauled my shirt off. The mosquitoes were going to have a fast food feast-out on my belly meat, but I didn't give a good goddamn. I tried to wrap the shirt around Tyree's wrist stump to bind it up. He kept waving the arm around, like a branch shimmying in the wind, flailing around like all of the bones in his arm had gone to rubber. It was like trying to splint up a broken Stretch Armstrong action doll with a couple of soggy popsicle sticks.

"Damn it, Tyree. Damn it. I'm so sorry."

I kept wrapping the shirt around the wound, but the damned thing kept coming loose. You couldn't really call what Tyree had a wound, anyway. It was something way bigger than a wound. It was like a door into his life, and everything was running out, and we were the three fuckers who had opened the door in the first place.

I felt somebody beside me. I looked around. It was Donny, kneeling like an altar boy at prayer.

"I'm sorry too, Tyree. I'm sorry we killed you."

He took out what he'd saved from the bear and pushed it onto Tyree's stump. I heard the bear meat suckling onto the wound like the pucker of a fat man hickeying onto a well-cooked spare rib.

"Here," Donny said. "Take this. It'll give you strength."

I wasn't sure how that was supposed to make sense, but not a whole lot of this night was making much sense in hindsight. Of course hindsight was only good for looking out of your asshole and wasn't much of a replacement for a good pair of field glasses.

I wrapped the shirt around whatever Donny had torn from out of the bear and given to Tyree's arm, and it seemed to stick the shirt on solid, like the best kind of Crazy Glue. I felt the shirt moving in and out in my hand, like the wound was breathing through the bit of bear.

"Here," A voice grumbled from above the three of us. For a moment I thought it was the bear, come back from the dead to set things right.

I looked up. Irvin was standing over us. He was holding out a pack of cigarettes like he was getting set to offer a smoke.

"There's got to be tobacco if you're making medicine with the dead."

He shook the cigarettes loose and crumpled them one by one, making a broken kind of circle about what was left of Tyree. I saw a fleck of the tobacco spackle onto the left of Tyree's lip. A part of me wanted to flick the damned thing away, but another part that knows enough not to whisper in church or whistle at a funeral told me to keep my hands the hell to myself.

"I'm sorry for killing you too, Tyree," Irvin said, and it felt like he really meant it.

Tyree's eyes sort of half-focused up towards Irvin. I could feel something between the two of them, like the two of them were chained in thin air.

"I didn't do it," Tyree whispered. "I didn't kill your brother, Irvin."

"I know you didn't," Irvin said. "I just wanted somebody to blame so bad that I looked around for anything in sight."

"It's all right," Tyree whispered. I had to lean closely to hear him. "Shit happens."

That last bit hit Irvin hard. It might have been easier if Tyree had just sworn at him or spit in his face. But letting go like that, letting go and not showing any sign of anger hit Irvin harder than a sixty car train wreck.

"Give me that pistol," Irvin said, taking it from me.

I don't think I could have stopped him if I'd wanted to. It was kind of irrevocable. It just had to be, you know what I'm saying? It was kind of like gravity and rain falling down. That gun just left my hands and passed into Irvin's, like it was something that just had to be.

I looked up at him, standing there over the three of us – me, Donny and Tyree. He could have shot us all, if he'd wanted to. He might even have been able to do it with one bullet, we were bunched up that close together.

Only he didn't.

He raised the pistol up towards the air.

"Goddamn you, God," He said low and gravelly, and then he fired three more shots straight up into the air. I don't know if he was trying to hit something or not.

"There's magic in threes," Irvin said. "There are three fates, and three sides to every story, and three stooges, depending on how you count."

I don't know if Irvin was conjuring or cursing.

"Give me that Luger back," I said.

Irvin looked at me. "You scared I'm going to shoot you?"

"I want to shoot one, too. For Tyree."

He handed it to me, butt first. "There are only two shots left."

"One's all I need," I said.

I held the Luger up to the sky. It felt heavier than it ought to, like it was freighted down with something a little more than bullets. Then I fired it, just once.

It seemed louder than before. Maybe my ears were just hearing it better.

It seemed to take forever for the sound of the single shot to fade away.

When the echo had vanished, Tyree had stopped breathing. I set the Luger down beside him. There was nothing there but the three of us standing in the darkness, listening to the mosquitoes buzz.

"We got to eat some of him, too," Irvin said.

I didn't argue. I lit a fire. Donny just watched.

Irvin got his hunting knife out.

"You want something from his leg?" He asked.

"I sure don't want rump roast," I answered.

Irvin finished carving. The whole proceeding had a kind of ceremonial feeling to it, like a last supper or a midnight church picnic. "Let's take our time and build us a good bed of coals and cook this up right."

"Daylight's coming soon," I pointed out.

Irvin just looked at me.

"I seen the light," He said. "Are you going anywhere too soon?"

I shook my head.

Irvin looked at Donny.

"Why don't you go on home, Donny. Somebody needs to get that truck back to the shop."

Donny stared.

"I want to stay and eat with you."

Irvin shook his head.

"We'll eat some for you," Irvin said. "You run along now, and get that truck back, before I get pissed at you."

"You're always pissed, Irvin."

Irvin grinned at that.

"Not anymore," He said.

Donny wandered off. I watched him walking away. A part of me wondered if maybe he hadn't set the hotel fire. He hadn't really said that he didn't. You never could tell with Donny.

I'd be fucked if it mattered that much to me anymore.

"You think he'll find his way back to the truck?" I asked.

"If he doesn't he can follow the track. One way or the other it'll lead him somewhere."

The fire was growing.

"Do you think he did it?" I asked. "Started the hotel fire?"

Irvin shrugged. "It doesn't matter that much, any more."

He looked at me like he was sizing me up.

"You don't have to stick around either," Irvin said. "This wasn't your idea."

I shrugged.

"I'm hungry," I said. "I'll stay and get my fill."

Irvin nodded.

We watched the fire. For a while we could hear the sounds of Donny crashing through the woods.

Then, even that passed.

"Too bad we didn't bring us some marshmallows," Irvin said.

I laughed at that.

"So what do you think happened?" I asked.

"Happened with what?" Irvin asked.

"With the Hotel. What do you figure started the fire?"

Irvin looked out into the woods. I had the feeling he was looking at something, listening to it.

"Damned if I know," he said.

"Don't you even care?"

"Fuck," Irvin said. "Gilbert was always an asshole. I never did care much for him. He was just my brother, was all. He was someone I looked up to, because there wasn't anyone else around. And now there's nobody."

He stared out into the darkness, looking at something that I couldn't see.

"That's just how it is," Irvin said.

He picked up the Luger and pointed it straight at his skull, all business. "Shit happens, and then you die."

Before I could stop him he'd fired the last shot. I felt another baptismal spatter of warm jelly and bone bits slapping the other side of my face. If I'd been sitting a little closer I might have got caught by the bullet.

Irvin fell like a sack of meat with his legs still crossed Indian-style. He looked peaceful lying there, almost content.

I looked at him.

"If you think I'm eating your sorry ass, you've got another think coming," I said.

I added a bit more fuel to the fire and I slowly roasted a chunk of Tyree. I said my respects and chewed slowly. As I chewed I could hear the bear brains and Irvin's brains arguing back and forth across my skull bone, staking out their claim. I figured they each had an argument to share.

I added a few more sticks to the blaze. The flames leapt higher, crawling out of the circle of the rocks and tobacco and into the hush of the dead pine needles.

I sat there quietly watching the flames grow, getting larger and larger until they reached out and touched everything.

THE END

A NOTE FROM STEVE VERNON

Some folks like to say that I am a storyteller. Some folks say that I was born with a campfire burning at my feet. Some folks will even SWEAR that the word "boring" does not exist my personal vocabulary - unless I'm maybe talking about termites or ice augers.

Some folks say an awful lot of foolishness, don't they?

As for me – all I want to tell you is how intensely grateful I am that you actually pulled a few dollars out of your pocket and BOUGHT and READ this yarn of mine – because without readers like you I would be nothing but some sorry-looking bozo rattling away on a keyboard in some dark alley – on account of I didn't remember to pay the rent.

If you LIKED the book that you just read drop me a Tweet on Twitter – @StephenVernon - and yes, old farts like me ACTUALLY do know how to twitter – and let me know how you liked the book – and I'd be truly grateful.

If you feel strongly enough to write a review, well that's fine too. Reviews are ALWAYS appreciated – but I know that not all of you folks are into writing big long funky old reviews – so just shout the book out just any way that you can – because I can use ALL the help I can get.

Now - If you liked HAMMURABI ROAD, you might want to try...

Sudden Death Overtime : A Tale of Hockey and Vampires

Prologue

In the beginning of the world there was no death.

No one knew the sorrow of that final ending.

No one knew the grief of losing someone they loved.

No one had tasted a single bitter tear.

The People grew fat and abundant.

Far too abundant.

The land grew crowded.

The food was harder and harder to find.

The People grew unhappy.

So the Great Raven looked down from his high-looking mountain and saw all this.

"This is a bad thing," the Great Raven said. "There is not enough food and water and land for the People to continue to live on in peace and harmony."

So the Great Raven decided that he would do something about this problem.

"I will create a gift so that the People can rise up and leave this world to make room for those who will follow in their path."

And so the Great Raven – in his wisdom and his sorrow – created Death.

Tuesday night 9pm

No one noticed quite exactly when the long black bus stole into the parking lot of the Anchor Pub. As far as anyone knew the bus just sort of drifted into the Labrador coastal village of Hope's End like an unexpected snow flurry.

Things happen that way in the town of Hope's End.

Slow and unexpected and all at once.

Judith Two Bear leaned her elbows against the wood grain of the unvarnished table top. Her cigarette glowed like a lighthouse's lonely beacon, bobbing as she nodded three slow beats behind the music of the static-ridden radio. She had parked herself at the window seat since dinner time. She liked to watch the world go by from the sanctuary of the town's only drinking hole – the Hope's End Drink and Drop Tavern and Grill.

Several long slow warm beers later Judith Two Bear found herself staring vaguely at the names and dates carved and inked into the table top. She knew some of them. She could guess at some of the others and she wondered just who the hell the rest really were. How many lonely souls had made their mark on this table and had then just sat here like so many half-finished glasses of warm draft beer – just waiting to be swallowed but not quite yet.

Truthfully, she didn't think of any of this.

Not in those exact words, anyway.

People don't really think that way – only in books and poetry and movies and other such bullshit. Rather, Judith Two Bear felt it, perhaps. She breathed it in with the stale pub air. Her grew her own sort of loneliness, nursing her drink and her evolving disappointment and her unvarying boredom that were as much a part of her as was the blood that sludged through her tired veins.

Nothing was left.

She had lived her life and had nothing but time left to her lonely keeping. She had seen her kids grow up and run away, her lovers grow cold and run away, she had seen life pull up to the curb and wave gaily once or twice before passing her right on by.

Her hands weighed heavy on the scarred pine tabletop. Her knuckles were cracked and leathered like old alligator skin, tattooed with nicotine and age. Her eyes had grown dull and nothing that hinted of girlhood was left to her save a shotgun blast of freckles playing hide-and-seek within the wrinkles and worry-lines that troughed down her cheeks like a memory of tears.

She stared at her flat beer.

The time drifted past the hope of anyone offering to take her home for any other reason but pity. Fergus McTavish had said he'd see her here, but so far he hadn't showed. She believed he'd only told her that to be kind. Fergus McTavish was a good man, after all, although he spent far too much time out there on that damned hockey rink with old Sprague.

What in God's frozen earth did grown men see in the rattle of sticks, the slashing of steel over ice and hockey sweaters worn way beyond funk?

Judith Two Bear sat there, disinterestedly listening to the soft current of gossip prowling through the Drink and Drop Tavern; folks wondering just where the black bus came from. Perhaps it was a fresh oil rig crew, or perhaps a wandering rock band. Perhaps a pack of tourists, far off course, with their pockets jingling with cartwheels of American silver and the promise of better days.

Judith Two Bear knew better.

No one in their right mind would ever WANT to come to Hope's End, Labrador where the only thing that kept the town going was the influx of oil rig workers who stopped here between shifts to get drunk and fed and laid; the three weeks of seal hunters who would stop here to get drunk and fed and hopefully laid; and the occasionally dangled promise of incoming government money.

There were a lot of them - so many promises washed up like waves on the rocky beach, only to be pulled away just as fast.

She stared at her beer.

The lights dimmed as the town generator kicked up a notch.

The last tune on the jukebox crackled out, only to be replaced by another goddamn hockey game.

Judith Two Bear stood up carefully.

Fergus McTavish wasn't coming, she decided.

She laughed to herself.

There had never been a hope that he would come.

Life doesn't really work that way.

Love is nothing more than a lie told in a midnight poker game where everyone cheated and nobody truly won.

She leaned backwards and listened to the creaks and cracks in the fossil that her doctor laughingly referred to as a spinal column.

The evening had passed as slowly as a yearlong bout of chronic constipation.

Time had moved inexorably.

Judith Two Bear was six beer older – without a candle to show for it.

Maybe seven beer – who the fuck really counted?

The television commentator shouted as someone banged the puck home. A few onlookers moaned and someone listlessly cheered. No one noticed as Judith emptied her glass of warm beer and turned it bottom-up on the table top.

She walked out the front door.

It was cold for a January evening. She pulled her shawl about her, holding it close. The shawl was the last gift that Little Whalen Pinto had given to her before he'd got drunk five months ago and had fallen from the ferry, halfway home to Newfoundland.

Whalen Pinto had washed ashore three days later. The current had carried him to the beach, shrouded in seaweed and picked at by the gulls. There were nights when Judith nightmared over Whalen Pinto's tide-swollen memory, the tears drowning in the memories his eyes, a crab picking listlessly at a bit of unfingered ear wax.

Other nights she dreamed of him singing - tone deaf and lustily bawling out that old Gordon Lightfoot standard, "The Wreck of the Edmund Fitzgerald", over and over – the only tune he knew straight through. The nightmares were her only company these days. She welcomed them as a lonely woman welcomes the nightly visit of a phantom lover.

"Damn it," she swore at the shadows.

She had truly hoped that Fergus McTavish would have shown tonight. She had hoped that he would replace her memories with a little actual companionship.

But Fergus wasn't coming.

"God-be-Jesus damn it."

The wind was cold in the parking lot.

There were only a few cars. Most people lived close enough to walk.

The black bus loomed in the darkness. There was no other word for it. It loomed – like the shadow of a mountain cast over a lonely gray tombstone.

It was heavy.

Solid.

Black and implacable.

For just a half an instant Judith Two Bear felt the urge to turn and run back into the pub and scream her panic – drowning out the hockey game and the clink of beer bottles and the tired rattle of conversation.

But what the hell would that accomplish?

She drifted a little closer to the black bus – as if she wanted to prove something to herself.

This close she saw that the windows were painted over.

Even the front window, all black.

How could a driver see his way through the night?

It might have been one-way glass, she supposed. You could see out, but nobody else could see in. But it looked more like the window glass had been spray painted over. All black, as if something were trying to hide. A part of her wanted to run from the bus and the parking lot but she was too tired to listen.

She leaned over and gently touched the side of the bus.

She felt a rhythm, like a tide, like a heartbeat, throbbing within the strange blackened walls of the vehicle.

Music, perhaps?

Her hand sank inwards into the cold black paint, like she was reaching into a basin of cold black water. Then she leaned a little deeper. Something purred, deep within the color of the bus. Something purred and something drew her in. She felt the color of the bus inhaling – like an old man sucking in his last puff of cigarette smoke.

Judith Two Bear's knees buckled slightly.

Her skin paled and the paint on the bus greedily darkened.

She could see the grill and headlights grinning at her. She wondered just how that was possible. She was leaning on the side of the bus, nowhere close to the grillwork. She shouldn't have been able to see it.

She didn't care.

Fergus wasn't coming.

She leaned there against the bus, allowing whatever was hiding inside it to drink its fill.

She wasn't trapped - only comfortable.

The bus door grated open.

Judith Two Bear drew her hand from the lulling cloy of the paint and freely entered the bus, still dreaming of the Edmund Fitzgerald.

The bus door closed behind her. If there was any screaming it was drowned in the lonely swallow of a North Canadian night sinking home. It began to snow, soft fat flakes that promised a hard storm to come. The snowflakes melted and slid across the grinning grillwork of the night-dark bus.

Fergus McTavish showed up at the tavern, one hour too late.

(if you want to read the rest of this vampire/hockey novella you REALLY need to order yourself a copy from your favorite book or e-book distributor)

And – if you are a glutton for punishment you might want to have a look at this excerpt from my full length novel of pure scarecrow terror!

TATTERDEMON

PROLOGUE - SUMMER 1691

Preacher Abraham Fell stared down at the witch Thessaly Cross, breathing like he'd run for a good long stretch. He leaned over, bending at the knees to lay another slab of fieldstone upon her chest.

"We beat you with hickory and we beat you with iron," he said. "And you have withstood every blow."

He stooped down and picked up another rock, never taking his eyes off her, as if she were some kind of dangerous viper who might strike at any moment.

He set the next rock on top of her, directly beside the others.

"We shot you and the musket balls swerved in midair like they were afraid of sinking into the taint of your flesh."

He scooped up another rock, grunting as he scooped. He just wasn't as young a man as he used to be – and no wonder.

Sights like this one aged you faster than years ought to run.

"We hung you in a noose woven from a widow's gray hair, a noose soaked in children's tears and you kicked and cackled like a hell-kite in the wind."

He laid the next rock down, sank to his knees and scooped up another stone. He was building a kind of rhythm that made the labor just a little easier.

"We burned you but even fired failed us."

It was true. She had witched a storm from a cloudless sky and drowned the blaze cold. Young Seth Hamilton, the town smith who had been the only man to dare kindle her pyre had been cindered black.

"Let the stones crush you and the dirt eat you," Fell said, laying another rock – which made thirteen stones in all. These were all good sized stones, hand-picked, at least the weight of child's corpse. She ought to have been crushed by the weight upon her yet she carried the load as if it were nothing but sticks and straw.

"Where did you hide the broom, witch?" Fell asked.

"Maybe it's up your bunghole," Thessaly taunted. "Have you looked there recently?"

The broom was her power and Fell feared it – although he knew that he shouldn't have. It was just a thing of woven willow. His grand-nanny swept the pine boards of her cabin daily with just such a broom and she certainly wasn't a witch.

Wasn't she?

He bent for another stone.

Thessaly spat in his face. "Bury that, god kisser."

He dropped the fourteenth stone upon her. It made a hard sound, like the witch Thessaly had stared too long at the Gorgon. He grunted at the effort and she laughed at his strain – which stung his pride hard.

"You must pay for your crimes against God and this community," Fell said.

Thessaly snorted. It wasn't any kind of human sound. Her snort sounded heavy and animalistic - like that of a boar in rut.

"What I pay for is refusing to give you my land," she pointed out, as the wind rattled the grass. "What I pay for is witching your field in return for your greed. I pay for your cattle that ate the gray grass. Happiest of all, I pay for your daughter, Fell."

Eliza.

Damn it.

Fell could still taste the smell of the dead meat festering in the back of his sinuses. He had put down the last tainted beast this morning. He had beaten it square in the skull with his best chopping axe. The metal of the blade had chewed into the bone and stuck hard. He had to put his left boot against the cow's forehead and lean back to work the axe loose. The unholy cattle hadn't moved, not one of them - even after he had cut the first two down. The cursed cattle had just stood there in his field, the wind making slow soft harp sounds blowing through their gray rattled guts.

He had put his daughter Eliza down before he had started with the cattle. Then he burned what was left of her and he buried her ashes in the field.

The husk that he had burned and buried wouldn't have nourished a worm.

"Was the milk tasty, Fell?" Thessaly taunted him. "Did young Eliza find it sweet?"

"Witch!" Fell hissed.

He snatched up a skull-sized rock scraping his hand against the rough granite and marking it with his own blood. He would match his stone and his blood against hers, he fiercely swore.

But first he had to know.

"Where did you hide the broom?"

"Closer than you imagine."

She spat again. The phlegm spattered the grass. The wind blew a little harder as Fell flung the stone. The granite chipped and sparked upon her flesh.

The farmer in Fell's soul feared a run of wildfire. A spark could easily rise up in dry times like this and tear through an entire countryside.

"I'll curse you Fell. I'll curse you and all those who stand with you." the old woman began to chant. "Merry through the prickle bush, the gore bush, the hump; careful round the holly fall, she'll catch your shadow hold...,"

The onlookers stiffened like a pack of wintered over scarecrows. Fear, or something darker, rooted their feet to the earth. Fell stumbled back from the pit. The wind stiffened and gusted as Thessaly laughed all the harder.

"Our father," Fell began to pray. "Protect us from this harridan's evil spells."

Thessaly continued to laugh.

"It is no spell, you fool. It is nothing more than a children's rhyme, Fell. It was only a nursery rhyme. Maybe I wasn't witching your field. Maybe I was merely waving my broom at a thieving crow."

Did she speak the truth?

Fell smothered his doubt.

Thessaly Cross had killed Eliza and Abraham Fell would not rest until he saw the witch finally dead.

He knelt down and caught hold of the next stone.

Only she wouldn't stay quiet.

"Witches don't curse, Fell. Only men curse," Thessaly ranted. "They curse themselves and their pitiful lot."

"You lie," Fell said, working the stone free

"Truth! I tell truth. Witches dance in easy circles. We follow the rhythms of time and tide and the wind that washes the earth's bones dry."

The wind howled. A tangled snare of root rammed through the dirt. Fell stepped back too late. The root twisted like a snake. It snared Fell's wrists and held him fast.

"Witches plant what men water with tears," Thessaly shrieked. "Witches sow the sorrow men must reap. Know this, Fell. When you harm a witch you plant a grudge as old as regret."

Fell tugged against the root. From the corner of his eye he saw the rest of the townsfolk, snared like screaming rabbits.

"I have you Fell. I have you all. Now you will see what a witched field really is."

And then Thessaly set the field to work.

She stirred dead grass into unholy life. The strands and stalks whirred like a wind of teeth, slicing through men and women who tried too late to run away.

The first man died in mid-scream, as a gust of grass harrowed the meat from his bones. A root, flung like a dirty javelin, impaled a second man. A third went down beneath an airborne avalanche of fieldstone.

The wind grew gray with dust, straw and flesh. The earth opened in great cratered swallowing mouths.

The townsfolk all died screaming.

Only Fell remained.

He stared at the carnage, as helpless as a snared rabbit.

"Witches sow, Fell. Witches sow and men must reap."

She raised her hands.

He saw gray dirt imbedded beneath her fingernails.

"Shall I tell you where I have hid my broom, Fell? Have you guessed? Do you really want to know? I buried it in your very own field."

The broom rose straight up from the earth's dirty womb, not more than an arm's reach from Fell.

"I and my broom will wait for you, Fell. We will wait for you like a seed waits for rain. Live with this. I have taken every one you know, but I let you live to breed. I let you live with the knowledge that one day I will return to visit your descendants."

Fell braced his feet in the dirt. He prayed for the strength of Samson. He fought against the root.

"Now I will show you how to bury a witch," she crowed.

She hugged herself as if hugging an unseen lover. The earth moved in reply as a thousand rocks flew from the flesh of the field and hovered above her homemade grave. Fell tore his wrists from the shackle of root.

He felt the skin rip from his bones.

"No descendants! No curse! Today we die together," he howled.

He uprooted the broom with his freshly skinned hands. He threw himself down upon her. His momentum drove the broom handle straight through her heart. A gout of stinking blood splashed his face.

The willow twig head of the broom stood out in all directions like an angry star. Fell saw the flash of tiny unimaginable teeth grinning from the end of each writhing twig.

Then the broom took him.

It ate at his face like his skin was nothing more than apple rind. He felt the white-hot twig-worms gnaw his features. He felt them tear and burn through the bowl of his skull. They crawled into the jelly of his brain and nibbled at his thoughts.

He had time for one last scream.

The broom ate that as well. It swallowed each morsel of Abraham Fell's pain and terror as it dragged him deeper down into the hole with the witch. The rocks poised above them like a pair of hands, ready to applaud. Thessaly pushed him from her. She nearly pushed him from the grave.

"Live, Fell. Let the meat grow back upon your opened skull. Crawl back from the brink of death. My curse shall stand. This earth grows too cold for me. I will wait for you and your descendants in the belly of hell."

"No!" Fell pushed back down upon her. "The curse ends here."

He shoved forward. He felt the broom slide and suck through the cage of his ribs. He pushed himself closer, impaling himself on the broom handle. The willow wood splintered inside him. It nailed him to Thessaly's twisting frame. He felt her bones wiggling beneath her meat like worms in the dirt.

She nearly slipped free.

He bit her lip, tearing grayish meat. The pain racked her concentration. She let her spell and the rocks above them drop. The grave, the broom, the witch and Fell were sealed in completely.

For a long time, nothing moved.

The moon rose like a slow ghost, lanterning down upon the butcher field.

A small gray form pushed from the rocky grave. The gray hairless skin glistened beneath the cool wash of moonlight, like the hide of a stillborn rat.

It crawled away into the darkness that surrounded the field.

A lone owl hooted remorselessly.

...soooon...

CHAPTER ONE - Three Hundred Years Later

* 1 *

I'm going to die, Maddy thought.

And the whole thing is all my fault.

She stared at her reflection in the dark kitchen window and her dead mother's eyes stared back at her. There was a question asked in those ghost window eyes.

What are you going to do now, girl?

Maddy couldn't say.

Vic stood in the center of the kitchen, waving his arms like a one-man windmill. Zigger slunk beneath his feet, gazing up with eyes pale as rotted moons, hoping to be fed.

Again.

"What the hell were you thinking?" Vic yelled.

Maddy felt her bones reaching down through the floorboards into the Nova Scotian dirt. She felt her bones take root, going to seed. What had she been thinking? She should have run a half a dozen years ago.

Now she was trapped.

Just like her mother.

Vic kept yelling, one of the only things he was good at. "I come home a little late and you do a thing like this. What were you thinking?"

Maddy didn't regret what she'd done, just doing it so stupidly. She'd been angry. She should've known there'd be trouble. She told herself that she needed to keep just as calm as possible.

She watched her reflection as she answered.

"A little late? It's nearly midnight. You could have phoned."

"The payphone at Benson's was broke. Somebody buried a goddamn slug in it."

Vic always had a ready lie. Lord but she was tired of it. She was tired of a lot of things. Marriage with Vic had started out fun, but fun changed fast. Vic grew mean just as soon as he had his cubic zirconium leash planted on her finger.

"You weren't at Benson's," Maddy said. "You were at the tavern, spending your pay check. You probably danced yourself a couple of go-rounds with the shortest skirt in the place, I bet."

Vic grinned, knowingly.

He was such a total bastard.

He didn't even try to hide it.

"A man's got a right to relax. Besides, I was at Benson's, having a cup of coffee."

She was tired of arguing, but what else could she do? Divorce him? She couldn't expect any alimony. Vic would just laugh and drive away and that would be that – which would leave her on meant welfare.

No way.

She'd be cold in the ground before she'd lean on the dole.

"I smell bourbon," she remarked and instantly regretted it.

Vic's eyes flattened like slices of cut glass.

Maddy had just stepped over the line.

"Maybe your nose is broke and you smell things wrong," he suggested. "It could happen."

Stupid.

She hadn't planned to make him angry. She should have stopped right then and there - only she didn't feel like stopping.

She made herself loose and ready to duck.

She usually could dodge the first couple of swings.

"You could have phoned," she argued. "It's a public restaurant. You could have asked Jack to use the counter phone. He wouldn't have minded."

Vic bulldozed straight through her argument. "Don't talk goddamn foolishness, girl. Jack Benson never lets anyone use that phone, not unless the kitchen was burning down."

"You could have tried."

"Never you mind. Me being late is no excuse to do what you done."

"It had gone cold," she explained for the dozenth time.

"Well what's a microwave for?"

"The microwave was broke, just the same as the pay phone."

He nearly laughed. It was too bad he didn't. It would have been over but out of the blue old Zigger started to bark. Vic booted the hound square in the ribs. The dog yelped in protest.

"Shut up hound."

Kicking the dog should have cooled him down only Vic never worked that way. A little violence stirred him up like a poker shoved in a fire.

"I just need to know what you were thinking," he asked, coming back to his anger like a dog after a bone. "Doing a thing like that."

"It went cold," she repeated. "It went cold, I was tired and it was near midnight. The dog needed feeding. If you'd put some dog food in the house like I asked, I wouldn't have had to give him yours."

"There was a hockey game on," Vic argued. "Can't you understand?"

His voice rose at the last like a hurt little boy. Maddy nearly laughed. He was just so dense. He couldn't realize what an absolute shithead he was being. She nearly laughed, but laughter right now would have been too much like asking for it.

She wasn't suicidal.

Not yet.

She tried to make peace.

"Look Vic, there's a stick of salami in the fridge if you want. Some pickles and relish if you'd like. I'd be glad to fry you up a couple of slices and make you a sandwich of it."

"I don't want no stinking salami and I'm sick to death of your preserves. I want my supper, damn it, and I want it now."

From beneath the table's safety, Zigger barked again. He was always going off, ever since his eyes went. His baying bounced off the ratty gray walls of the kitchen until it seemed the plaster would shatter.

"Quiet!" Vic yelled, kicking at the table and the dog beneath it.

Don't let him get you going, she told herself, but there was something growing inside her and getting bigger as every moment slipped by.

"So I thought," Maddy started, still trying to figure how to change the subject.

That instant of lapsed attention was all Vic needed. He grabbed her by the chin and twisted her face around to meet his gaze.

"Thought what Maddy? What'd you think? What have you ever thought in your godforsaken life?"

He pushed his face close to her, looming over her. He really didn't need to. Vic was large all over, a totem of a man, all forehead and chin framed in a thicket of dark tangled hair. It made Maddy feel small, just standing next to him. It was a kind of slow erosion working away deep in her soul. Every year Vic made her feel a little bit smaller, like he was whittling her down until she was nothing but a shadow.

Some days she felt like she was nothing more than a puppet, dancing on his strings.

"If you learned how to think, then I sure want to know about it." Vic went on.

The thing got bigger inside her. Every breath cut like a fish knife, her heart banged like a crazy drummer. It's a heart attack, she thought. I'm having a heart attack.

"Maddy? Are you listening to me?"

Oh god I'm glad it's over. He can bury me where ever he wants to.

I don't care.

Zigger bayed and skittered across the tile floor.

"Shut up hound," Vic snarled. "It's bad enough you ate my goddamn supper."

Maddy squeezed her eyes shut. She felt a burst of blue light open like fireworks going off inside her skull.

Oh god.

It's a stroke, she thought. A stroke or a heart attack or maybe some sort of aneurysm.

Whatever it was it couldn't be any worse than life with Vic.

Just then Vic snapped his fingers a half inch from Maddy's eyes, calling her back from the brink of her imagined death.

"Hey!" he shouted.

Maddy opened her eyes, startled to attention.

"Are you listening?"

She stared. It wasn't a heart attack, but it sure was something. A blue dot of light popped open in front of Vic's chest. Maddy knew that the blue light had to have come from somewhere inside her. It wasn't anything she thought. It was more something that she just felt.

The dot hovered over Vic's heart, flickering like a blue firefly.

"Well?"

She saw her chance and she took it.

"It went cold, Vic. Your supper went cold and the pork chops were greasy and I figured you were out at Benson's and it's a restaurant so you must have had yourself some supper, now didn't you?"

The cavalry rode in just that quickly. She shifted the blame to him. She put him on the defensive. It would work. She had trapped him in his lie and made him feel like he had to hide the whole thing.

She'd beaten him again.

She didn't care. She didn't even notice, not really.

She was too busy staring at that blue light, wondering just what it was. Maybe the light wasn't from her. Maybe it was something else. One of those laser gun sights you saw in movies. What if there was a sniper out in the darkness of the field, taking aim on the kitchen? Getting ready to fire? Would it bother her, watching Vic get shot to pieces?

She decided to wait and see.

"Are you listening to me, girl?"

She nodded vaguely, entranced by the blue dot.

Vic rolled his eyes in disgust. "Wake up, hay-for-brains! Jesus Christ, you look like some kind of sleepwalker. Are you listening, hey?"

"I'm listening, Vic."

Only she wasn't listening at all. She hadn't been for years. Vic just had nothing new to say. As far as their marriage went he had stopped growing a long time ago.

The blue light widened. It was like staring at her Daddy's old television set, turning off in reverse.

"You ain't listening. Christ. For the life of me I don't know why I ever married you. Your Daddy was right, you know. You're stupid and ugly."

That hurt.

"I ain't ugly, Vic. Maybe I'm stupid, but I sure ain't ugly."

It was true. Maddy was always pretty. No movie star, mind you. She was a tough sort of pretty like a country weed in full bloom. Straw blonde hair, straight as a beggar could spit – with eyes that her Daddy used to call cornflower blue. A little gopher bump on the bridge of her nose, hooked down like a river running around a bend.

Thin in the flanks from work and worry, but living with Vic would do that to any woman.

"You're skinnier than a bean pole, and if them tits get any closer to the ground they'll leave skid marks where you walk."

That was a cruel truth. Maddy's knockers crept closer to her stomach every year. They nearly hid the row of five tiny circular scars Vic called her rib holes. But what could she do about that?

Nail them up?

"It's the law of gravity, Vic." she explained. "Sooner or later we all fall down. I can't help that. Nothing but trouble ever comes back up."

She stared at the blue dot, watching it grow. Vic didn't seem to notice the blue light at all, no matter how large it got. The dot started changing like it was taking shape.

"There you go again," Vic complained. "If you did some work around here instead of daydreaming, I might come home in a whole lot nicer mood."

That was a bold lie. Vic didn't know how to be in a good mood unless he was drunk and even that wasn't any kind of a guarantee.

The blue shape grew into a form. It looked like some kind of rag doll, getting bigger all the time. Vic thumped the pine table for emphasis. The salt and pepper shakers shivered in their wooden box.

Maddy didn't notice.

She was too busy staring at the hovering blue image directly between her and Vic.

The hovering blue image of her long dead father.

"How long are you going to let this skid mark with legs get away with that kind of crap?" Maddy's dead father asked.

(Yup, I know, I am teasing you again. But you can order the novel TATTERDEMON from your favorite book or e-book distributor)

My Regional Books – from Nimbus Publishing

Haunted Harbours: Ghost Stories from Old Nova Scotia
Wicked Woods: Ghost Stories from Old New Brunswick
Halifax Haunts: Exploring the City's Spookiest Spaces
Maritime Monsters: A Field Guide
The Lunenburg Werewolf and Other Stories of the Supernatural
Sinking Deeper OR My Questionable (Possibly Heroic) Decision to Invent a Sea Monster
Maritime Murder: Deadly Crimes From the Buried Past

My E-Books

Sea Tales
Flash Virus
Fighting Words
Tatterdemon
Devil Tree
Gypsy Blood
The Weird Ones
Two Fisted Nasty
Nothing to Lose – Captain Nothing, Volume 1
Nothing Down – Captain Nothing, Volume 2
Roadside Ghosts
Long Horn, Big Shaggy